The Truth About Trees

Deborah Dunleavy

To Fred, Enjoy each and every day. Deborah Dunleavy

Copyright © 2015 Deborah Dunleavy

All rights reserved. The use of any part of this publication reproduced, transmitted in any form or by any means, electronic, mechanical, photocopying, recording, or otherwise, or stored in a retrieval system, without written consent of the author - or in any case of photocopying or other reprographic copying is an infringement of copyright law.

This is a work of fiction and the characters in it are solely the creation of the author. Any resemblance to actual persons - with the exception of historical and popular figures is entirely coincidental. Similarly, some events and some geographies have been created to serve fictional purposes.

Cover Photograph by Linda Moir. Cover Model, Heather Savage.
FishOwl logo by Stephen Yeates.

ISBN: 1512214760
ISBN 13: 9781512214765
Library of Congress Control Number: 2015907953
CreateSpace Independent Publishing Platform
North Charleston, South Carolina

*For H.A.
forever and beyond*

*In memory of Lise Lilian
1953 - 2013*

I

Trees are poems that earth writes upon the sky,
We fell them down and turn them into paper,
That we may record our emptiness.

~Kahlil Gibran

1

SHE'D NEVER REALLY thought about it before. The roots, that is. How deep they go.

"They're as deep as this tree is tall," he had told her, "That's why they don't fall over unless there's a hurricane or they're dying or something."

Grace placed her head on Terry's shoulder. Her father would never miss the old blanket they were lying on. She'd taken it from the back seat of his beat up Buick. Above, the sun danced like diamonds on the leaves.

"You can make them look like a painting by Matisse." Grace squinted. "See, just squeeze your eyes and it gets all blurry and beautiful."

It was the first Saturday after her sixteenth birthday. The world smelled of lilacs and the warm air caressed their skin. Terry's hand stroked her arm, slow and sweet. His gentle touch made her face flush and her arms began to tremble.

"You're shaking Grace."

"I am not." The denial made it even worse. "I'm vibrating," she whispered.

Then Terry took her in his arms and she gave into the power. There beneath the protection of the oak tree, there on the ground that covered the mighty roots she gave him her heart, her psyche, and her soul.

She wrote poetry for weeks and nothing brought it back, that feeling of longing and loving.

By the end of the summer Terry had moved away. To some place on the other side of Toronto - Chatham or Windsor or some place like that. He was gone but her yearning for the experience seemed to last forever.

• • •

Grace knew she was dying. She might not remember what day of the week it was or whose birthday she had forgotten but one thing was for certain, - the lottery of life was coming to an end. This was the antithesis of the ultimate jackpot and she had won big time.

At fifty-six life seemed too damn short but there was no way that she was going to let on that she was really pissed off. This cancer thing was eating her up physically and emotionally but damned if anyone would know the truth.

"So it goes – nobody lives forever," she said to her doctor when he told her the tumor in her brain was inoperable. The "c" word had taken over her body. It was as if its tentacles were reaching out through every organism of her being and choking off what little was left of her.

He had taken away her driver's license. He said it was the seizures. She might have an accident and kill herself.

"Ah, hell, I'm going to die anyway," Grace joked. Faye, her older sister, didn't have quite the same sense of humor and ever since their parents had died she somehow felt responsible for even the things she couldn't control. Like cancer.

"Or someone else," Faye lectured, "you could hit someone."

The car was still in the driveway and Grace had stashed an extra set of keys in the wax paper roll. "Good thing I remembered that," she told the fridge as she made her plan to go quietly, to disappear, to leave no trace, to go back to the roots.

• • •

For weeks she tried to find it again – that moment of unspeakable bliss.

All that summer Grace walked through the woods to the same oak tree and looked for signs of their union. Maybe, she thought, maybe she'd find a coin or some sort of impression of their bodies on the ground. As if the heat of their bodies had singed the grass.

Once she even laid down in the exact position and tried to imagine his body next to hers. But it was too late. Time did not stand still. Time kept rolling on just like the rolling on the river song. She wanted to rewind that moment as if it were some old black and white movie she had seen at the cinema back when rock'n'roll was still alive, but it just couldn't be done.

Grace had tried to forget Terry. Writing poetry helped some days but whenever she read any of them to her mother who was at the height of menopause, all of her emotional creativity was dismissed.

"What are you writing about Gracie. It doesn't make any sense if you ask me. And turn the radio down will you."

Don't ask was the lesson learned. Don't ask a parent to understand. Don't ask anyone to understand the affairs of the heart. Don't ask. And God forbid don't tell.

• • •

Grace hadn't told anyone about her plans. Suicide by installment. Drinking oneself to death, was acceptable by society but suicide by exposure? You'd have to be crazy to do that. Grace knew she was forgetting things but she was definitely not crazy.

2

GRACE KICKED OFF her runners and piled her clothes on top of them hoping the ants wouldn't crawl into the pockets. She was completely naked. Looking down past her budding breasts she could see her pubic hair starting to grow. At 12 she had already had her first period. It was a killer.

"I'm ready. Are you ready?" Grace called out from behind the sumac trees that barely hid her body.

"Ready", Scott answered from the other side of the fallen elm they called the Kingdom of Zarra. Many acts of make-believe had unfolded in the land of the Great Elm but now for the first time they would step beyond fantasy into a prepubescent reality.

"You first," he called.

Grace was not so keen on being the first to reveal her nakedness but she really wanted to know what it looked like - Scott's penis. Last time she went to the dentist she saw a picture of the statue of Michelangelo's David in an art book on the table in the waiting room. Were all men the same?

All that August she said she would if he would and finally he agreed as long as he got to kiss her underwater the next time they went swimming. "Oh alright," she said. Kissing wasn't her idea of a good time. She was just curious that's all.

• • •

The first round of chemo had made her so sick she wished she were dead. At least Grace liked wearing hats and so when her hair fell out she had an excuse to go out and buy a few new ones. Make-up had never been part of her routine but she was invited by the volunteers at the hospital to give it a try. "It'll perk you up," they chorused. Grace looked in the mirror. In her mind the only thing missing was the embalming fluid.

A few weeks later her face puffed up like a butterball turkey. Even her best friend from high school didn't recognize her when she came to town to see her parents. They bumped into each other at Freda's Bakery.

"You, don't know me do you Janice?" Grace lined up behind her at the checkout.

Janice stood with her mouth open as if waiting for someone to toss her a butter tart.

"It's the chemo. Don't worry I'm not contagious."

"My God, Grace, I didn't know. Are you going to be alright? Is there anything I can do? I mean honestly after I see my folks at the retirement home I can come over."

Grace saw tears filling the corners of Janice's eyes. Oh no, mother of God, here we go again. Grace just couldn't handle another person freaking out over something that had nothing to do with them. Here it comes.

"I'm so sorry Grace."

What was the right response this time – Oh don't be, or me too, or it's not your fault, or for pity sake get over it will you.

• • •

The image of Scott's genitals haunted her for nights. She'd go to bed, turn off the light, close her eyes and there it was - all puny and wrinkled. It looked like an x-ray etched out against the darkness behind her eyelids.

She couldn't help laughing at him when they stood by the Great Elm. His privates looked weird, that's all. At least Scott never bothered to kiss her under water - or above for that matter. And at that moment of revelation the Kingdom of Zarra came to an end.

• • •

Everything was ready or as ready as it was going to be. Faye would get what little was left in her savings account plus the photo albums from summers up at the lake, not that her sister really liked the lake but Grace had to decide what to do with the photographs. She knew she couldn't take them with her to the other side. Nothing from the material world gets to leave on the death ship, Grace mused.

One morning, over a bowl of corn flakes, Grace pondered about her ancestors who had fled the famine infested villages and farms of Ireland. That was long before the days of photography. The summer after high school, she and a girl friend had gone to visit the graves of 5000 Irish who died in 1847 on Grosse Isle just up past Quebec City. The ships overflowed with rotting, stinking bodies. You could smell them long before you could see them, the Parks Canada interpreter had said.

They were lumber ships. They'd be loaded up with timber from the forests of Upper and Lower Canada. Once back in Ireland the ruthless owners of the fleets packed them with souls desperate to escape the oppression. It was a means of paying for the trip back. Dispensable cargo after all - that's what they were – the Irish.

• • •

All that August, before the bearing of their bodies, Grace and Scott staked out a fort beside the Great Elm. Each day they'd meet up and ward off the invisible invaders. The made swords from tree branches and buried their prized marbles as treasure right at the base of the elm. Sometimes Grace slew a dragon. And Scott gave out his impression of a Tarzan yodel. Sometimes they'd sit as still as statues in hopes that a bird might land on them. But by the end of the summer the world of fantasy had been erased by reality. There was no turning back and no more escaping into the Kingdom of Zarra.

• • •

Grace leaned against the basement wall and looked at the two boxes filled with the research she had done on the family trees. Her cousin's daughter on her mother's side would get the box marked Blair and the Ferguson's family tree would go to the genealogical society. She'd been a member there for the past three years. Maybe some distant relative would come by one day and all the work would be done for them.

Last week Grace had stuffed four garbage bags full of her clothes and called the clothing drive people to come and pick them up.

A day later a beat up blue van pulled into her driveway and a long haired young man rang the door bell. "Somebody die?" he asked.

"Nope. Not yet."

"Say what?"

"No one died."

3

WHEN DAVID WRAPPED his Harley around a tree they'd been living on the damp west coast for almost five years. That first summer their car broke down. They hitch-hiked just about everywhere - down into the interior to the parched lands of the Okanagan, then across Vancouver Island to the rain forests of Tofino beach. They even managed to sneak on the train that crossed over the Chilakoot Pass. Then when winter rolled in, they lucked out. A snowbird rented them a well used mobile home in Puce Coupe on the outskirts of Dawson Creek.

The following spring they hit the road again and managed to get a lift to the Queen Charlotte Islands with a pilot they met when they were hanging out a local bar in Prince Rupert. His name was Gary. He flew a Grey Goose for this guy who owned the paper mill up near Smithers.

David said he could build a house on Hippie Hill on the outskirts of Queen Charlotte City. And he did. He also built an open air squatter, and on those monster-cramp nights of Grace's menstruation, it was really a drag.

It all seemed to be a blur - those freedom years - like the way trees went into kinetic motion when David and Grace ripped through the mountain roads on his Harley, going ninety miles an hour - like the way Grace threw the oils against her canvas for weeks after the accident.

• • •

Grace perched herself on her 1940's vintage red wooden suitcase stuffing the bits of paper into the shredder. She had once weighed her sense of self worth by her collections of salt & pepper shakers and knick knacks from flea markets, but that all seemed sort of silly now.

A few weeks ago Grace had a message from the divine, at that moment where time does not exist, in that place between sleeping and waking. God had spoken over her cerebral PA system - you're born with nothing and you die with nothing - at least nothing from the Madonna's material-girl world.

The next day she took every doohiggy, whatchamacallit and thingamabob back to Angelo's Flea Emporium, the same row of falling down sheds that for the last twenty years managed to not topple over onto the lot of the abandoned Drive In Theatre or the "thee-ay-ter", as the locals call it.

The shredder grabbed at the bits of paper like a ravenous dog - high school newspapers, rough pencil drawings on bits of placemats, taxes dating back fifteen years, letters from old flames. Grace sighed and stared far into space, another one of her more recent empty moments, and then a flash of emotion. There's no need to be sentimental. She spoke to the floor and that's when she saw it, underneath a pile of high school essays – her first sketch book.

• • •

"Don't worry." *David grabbed the tent as Grace rolled her back pack onto the damp moss below the towering totems. Nobody ever comes to this part of Skidagit.*

Grace looked up to the carved faces of raven, wolf, and frog – the protectors of the clans – the guardians of the ancestors. A shiver raced up her neck and into the roots of her hair. The wind whistled through the branches playing a rustling anthem to the forgotten village.

They walked down to the beach to watch the sun sink slowly into the silver ocean and on their way back they gathered up bits of drift wood for the fire. Grace watched the sparks shoot high up into the night sky as David stirred the embers with a stick. A shower of sparks cascaded upward. Look, Grace pointed to the purple-black sky. We're creating the Milky Way.

Then silence. Grace was lulled by the feeling of being only a speck in the universe. It made her feel safe and humble, and nothing could ever take this moment away from her. Ever.

That night Grace was the master of their love making love. She howled a deep throated cry of ecstasy and collapsed naked on top of David. They fell asleep in that moment of being one.

In her dreams Grace was flying; she could feel herself rising out of her body and the sound of a thousand raven wings filled her head. Suddenly she was perched in the tree looking down through the nylon of their tent. With one eye she saw herself curled up in David's arms. And with the other eye he was gone.

• • •

Grace wiped the dust from the corners of the sketch book; it read Hippie Hill -1971. It had been years since she last had enough courage to look back at those early drawings. She knew what was inside.

Slowly her fingers opened the black cover to a page where a piece of cedar bark marked it just so. It was David, lying nude on the bed in their ramshackle house on the hill. He was on his side, facing the forest wallpaper, his back to her. Sound asleep he had been completely unaware that he was her object of affection and a model for her musings.

A tear splashed onto the page. As she tried to wipe it away she smudged the charcoal drawing of his feet. And for the first time in weeks a pain raced through her skull – a pain not unlike someone driving a nail through her forehead right to the back of her neck. Grace stumbled off the suitcase, dropped to her knees and then fell, convulsing on the floor.

4

MRS. CALLAGHAN STOOD stern faced in front of the grade one class. Grace thought she was ancient, as old as the one room stone schoolhouse with the date 1888 over the door. And this was October 1956. Grace would turn seven in May.

Her father had promised to get her a real two wheeled bicycle when she turned seven. He kept his promise that time. The bicycle was fire engine red with rainbow colored tassels that sparkled at the ends of the white handle grips. Grace clipped bits of paper with clothespins to the wheels. It sounded just like a motorcycle.

But school was not what her mother had said it would be like. "You'll meet lots of new children there," she said wiping her hands on her stained apron. "And everyone loves Mrs. Callaghan. Why, she was my grade one teacher too."

Grace did not love Mrs. Callaghan whose bulging neck bobbled over her tightly buttoned white blouse. Once a button was undone at the front and everyone could see Mrs. Callaghan's pointy bra. When Grace tried to tell her she was told, don't interrupt, and she had to stay on the sidewalk for a whole afternoon. No one was allowed to speak to Grace for the rest of the day.

So Grace drew pictures on the dirt with her finger. She got down on her knees and when she got home her mother scolded her for *getting dirty. No, school was nothing but trouble as far as Grace was concerned.*

• • •

The dehumidifier hummed loudly in Grace's head not unlike a swarm of bees.

Damn it. Damn it to hell. Grace rolled over onto her side and pushed herself up into a sitting position on the basement floor. She leaned over to look at the scrape on her left knee when a drop of blood from her nose splattered on to the cement.

Thank God Faye isn't here. She'd force me to go to emerge like the last time.

Having a seizure at the family barbeque was less than graceful and heaven knows Grace had already had a hard enough time living up to her name.

Slowly Grace stood up and smoothed out her cotton shirt and pants. Nothing broken, thank God. Cautiously she staggered over to the corner of the basement and leaned over to rest her body against her mother's old walnut dressing table. It had been there since she died in '98, the year her mother's heart had failed for the third and final time.

Grace looked in the mirror. Who was this woman? How had she become so changed, so sad, so much like her mother?

• • •

"You're just like your mother Grace Ferguson, red hair and the gift of the gab, now stop your chitter-chatter and draw those circles and lines. You'll learn to print better. Now get to work."

Circles and lines, circles and lines and infinity signs. Circles and lines, circles and lines and infinity signs. Grace's tiny hand retraced the infinity sign over and over again until the tip of her lead pencil almost went through the paper.

"What on earth is that?" Mrs. Callaghan loomed over Grace's desk. Grace didn't say anything. That was the safest thing to do since any time she did say something she ended up being put in the corner or told to stay on the sidewalk again.

"Is it a circle?"

Grace shook her head.

"A line?"

Again Grace shook her head.

"Well...."

"It's forever and ever."

"Oh is it now and how would you know anything about that. Now do what you're told to do."

Grace didn't know how she knew. It was one of the first times she realized she just knew some things that couldn't be explained. It was the same with spirals. They were much more fun to do than just circles and lines. And when her teacher caught her drawing spirals she was told not to doodle.

• • •

Grace pulled herself together. She held onto the railing on the stairwell and she slowly climbed her way up to the kitchen. Mint tea always seemed to soothe her after one of these stupid episodes. She put the kettle on and sat at the kitchen table. There was grocery pad with a picture of a cow on it. Grace picked up a pen and began to doodle triangles, starbursts, spirals, and her favorite, lemniscates – the sign for infinity.

• • •

Like a little candle burning in the night
In this world of darkness, so you must shine
You in your small corner
And I in mine

"Lillian." Grace's mother, tried to wake Grace up but she was locked inside her dream. She could hear her mother calling her name but she couldn't move. And Mrs. Callaghan was singing a wicked, evil song and holding a candle under her chin. She was a monster about to devour her.

That day Grace's father said she didn't have to take the bus to school. He would drive her all the way in his big, blue Pontiac. It was raining cats and dogs so they sang The Old Grey Mare and Catch a Falling Star to the beat of the windshield wipers.

From the school yard Grace watched as he drove away. The other children had already gone inside. Grace wanted to be a 'good girl' just like her father had told her to be. She wanted Mrs. Callaghan to like her.

Eagerly Grace dropped her Roy Roger's lunch box at the steps and ran over to the trees that lined the boundary between the school yard and the farm next door. There were thousands of autumn leaves – oak, maple, elm, poplar, chestnut. Her grandmother had taught her the names. And they were beautiful - colors that Grace had never seen in her crayon box – royal purple, shimmering yellow, golden orange. This would be her peace offering to Mrs. Callaghan.

• • •

The road map lay open on the dining room table. Grace flicked on the overhead light, and leaned over to look at her route. It was October so the provincial parks were closed and there had been a frost on the weekend. Now was the time to go, but where? Grace knew she wasn't up for a big hike. It had to be somewhere where she could stash the car and still be far enough off the beaten track. She didn't want to be found – at least not until the spring.

• • •

After the bell had been rung for the end of recess they found Grace crouched down under a pine tree at the edge of the school yard. She was *drenched from head to foot and covered in mud. Clutched in her hands was a bouquet of leaves — every color of the universe.*

Grace handed them to her teacher.

When they got back inside Mrs. Callaghan threw the leaves into the trash can in the classroom and Grace had to sit soaking wet in the cloak room until her father was called from his job at the plant to come and take her home. That was the first time Grace got the strap. And she was put to bed without dinner.

Grace's mother kissed her good night. In her eyes Grace could see the pain.

And after the rest of the house grew quiet Grace switched on the lamp on her dresser, tiptoed across the floor and pulled a bright red maple leaf from her school bag. She cradled it in her hands as she took it over to the lamp. Gently she held it up to the light; she could see all the veins spreading out in every direction. She could see right into the crimson cells and right into the endlessness of infinity.

In that moment of innocence Grace was overcome with complete wisdom. She was a traveler on a planet where everyone was in too much of a hurry to take the time to see or to be. None of this came to her in words. It was simply a knowing - a place of being alive.

5

IT WAS ON the Queen Charlottes that Grace seriously took up painting. In a secret sort of way that only David knew about, Grace dreamed of following the spiritual brush strokes of Emily Carr – to take over where she had left off – to capture the power of the trees whose branches swirled up to meet the face of God.

And it was at this time that David took to turning wood. He found rhythms and textures in the knots and crevices. Grace loved his work. And she loved David in a way that had no time – no before, and no after, but always.

And it was at this time on the Queen Charlottes that Grace and David decided to give up birth control and have a baby. But a baby would not have them. The tears flowed. They were young he said, there's plenty of time. And he rocked her like a boat on the ocean, so great was his love for her.

• • •

When Grace came out of the attack Faye was sitting on the linoleum floor, cradling Grace's head on her lap.

"Sh. Sh. It's alright. Everything's going to be alright."

The kitchen light stung the back of her eyeballs as she tried to look at her sister's face. She was too weak to speak. Having two seizures in a row had zapped every ounce of her strength.

Faye had dropped by with some groceries and to check in as usual, like she did every Tuesday afternoon, like clockwork, like a mother cat whose kittens have been taken away.

"You've got to make a choice Grace. Either you come and stay with us or you go to a place, a facility...." Faye could not bring herself to say nursing home.

Deep down Faye knew she couldn't save her sister's life. And she couldn't save her father's when on the eve of the first man walking on the moon he died from poisoning his liver, the result of losing his job and drinking too much for too many years.

• • •

Grace and Faye stood solemnly on either side of their mother. Faces without names said they were sorry, what a tragedy, he was a good man.

Countless memories raced through Grace's mind. The tree fort he built her when she was nine, the day he stopped talking to her because he found out that she and Scott had revealed themselves to each other, the nights he'd piss on the floor because he was too drunk to find the bathroom. Why did loving someone have to hurt so much?

After the funeral Grace told her mother that she wasn't going to go back to the College of Art in Toronto.

"Your father wouldn't want you to quit. Don't worry sweetheart, I'll be fine. Besides, Faye and Kent are only ten minutes away. You go, you hear, you go." And then she ran to her room and slammed the door. Grace leaned her head against the pine door and listened to the muffled sound of her mother sobbing into the pillow.

• • •

Tears welled up in her eyes. A flood of emotions swelled around her throat. It was the aftershock of the seizures. Grace sat at the kitchen table. Everything was out of focus, her vision, her mind...

"You alright?"

"Yeah, I'm fine. Fine."

Here drink this. Faye passed her a cup of cold mint tea that was still sitting on top of the map of Ontario. Just then Grace's hand made a sudden jerk spilling the green liquid all over the table, the map, and Faye's shoes.

Faye didn't say a word. It wasn't the first time that Grace had had a spastic moment. Quietly she ripped off some paper towel and started mopping up the mess.

"Why have you got the map out?"

Shit! Grace said to herself. What should she say? She was reliving old road trips, like the time they went to the provincial park and almost got struck by lightning?

"Remember the time we went to the park up north and got hit with lightning?" Faye took the thought right out of Grace's head. Or had Grace seen the thought in her sister's head. They were like this now and again. Psychic sisters.

"Yeah, that was freaky, really close. You could feel the electricity in the tent." Grace pulled her graying hair back off her forehead.

"So?" Faye put one hand on her hip and pointed to the map with the other hand. "What's the scoop?"

Fibbing was not an art that Grace had mastered in her life but she had to do it and she hoped that her sister's psychic antennae were down. "I've decided to go to a retreat, for a week or so," Grace said without really thinking it through.

"You've what! I mean Grace look, you've just had another seizure."

Grace turned and walked toward the living room. There was no way Grace would tell Faye that this seizure had been a double whammy. And she definitely would not say what her inner voice was really thinking.

"So?" Faye called from the kitchen.

"I may never have another chance, and damn it Faye, I deserve it, and you're not going to stop me. You're not. Besides, I've already bought my bus ticket."

6

HER MOTHER HAD convinced her. She would go back to college, though in her heart she felt somehow conflicted. Was it the anger from her father dying before she could make peace with him? Or was it that some part of her really resented everything about him and the guilt of this knowing blotted out all other rational reason.

Grace enrolled in her classes but she spent more time skipping out of them than actually going to them. The city had so much more to teach her - about life – about loneliness – about the way of being an artist.

She detested some of her profs. They were self indulgent long haired creeps who coerced the girls into doing nude fashion shows with weird music. "It's art," they said. "Screw that," said Grace.

One Saturday at a club on Spadina she danced with this tall, thin guy by the name of David. Between dances they drank dark beer and she talked about how Leonardo de Vinci secretly stole cadavers so that he could study anatomy. David said too many trees were being clear cut from the forests and that he was going to go tree planting in northern B.C., did she want to come along.

That night, the first night, they made love three times between midnight and six in the morning. "So," he said over toast and coffee at the donut diner, "I'm leaving for B.C. pretty soon. I've got a 62 VW bug. They always have jobs out there. Wanna come?"

"Sure. Why not?"

• • •

After Faye left, Grace put on the best of Joni Mitchell and sat down to the hum of her computer. Now that she had lied to Faye about going to a resort, she had to back up her plan. The search engine came up with pumpkins in the logo – cute. Grace had almost forgotten Thanksgiving dinner was planned for next Monday. Damn. She said she'd bring the yam and pineapple casserole. She scratched yams on a scrap of paper. Later she'd go to the store. For now she had to choose a resort and have proof of a reservation.

She typed in resorts + Ontario. The screen flashed a million choices. Navigating the internet had always been a chore for Grace even before her diagnosis but now the light seemed to trigger headaches and nausea.

Quick, she thought, let's find one…The Willow Tree Resort… trails….hot tub…indoor pool…three meals…all inclusive. Grace wrote down the one eight hundred number, hit the print button and made it to the toilet just in time to puke her guts out.

• • •

It took over a week to get from Toronto to the tree planting site just inside B.C. from the Alberta border. The first delay was because of a flat tire they got outside of Terrace Bay, a mining town in Northern Ontario. David thumbed a lift to the one and only garage in town. Grace stayed behind to look at Lake Superior and the sea of rock and trees that stood on the other side of the road.

A logging truck passed by and the backlash of grit and gravel nearly blew her down the embankment. When the dust settled she looked out *again toward the endless lake. The sun dazzled its light like sapphires on the waves. She softened her stare until the colors became separate and distinct – blue, grey, green, silver, black, pink – it was as if she were standing in the middle of a Lauren Harris painting – waiting to be captured by the motion in the strokes of his brush.*

By noon David had come back in a tow truck. He had the repaired tire and two lemon sodas. Back on the road, they toked-up all the way to Winnipeg.

• • •

Lately Grace had been forgetting things, silly things, like today, when she got to the store she had forgotten what she was supposed to buy. She checked every pocket for the shopping list. All she came up with was an opened roll of breath mints, a soggy piece of tissue, a rubber band, and a fortune cookie saying from the Lee Sing Chinese Restaurant: Sincerity is the way to heaven.

Heaven knows Grace was sincere about her decision to disappear but not yet for God's sake. She had to pick up something for Thanksgiving dinner. What the hell was she supposed to buy? The sliding doors opened and she saw it – a huge basket of yams.

"Hey there Grace. How's it going?" A man in greasy coveralls and a bag of potatoes under his arm walked up to Grace. "You remember me?"

Grace didn't.

"I'm Bill Thompson's brother." Bill Thompson's brother came up close, so close that Grace could practically taste the stale coffee and cigarettes in the back of her throat. She started to gag.

"Right. Say hi to Bill." Grace turned away and picked out a few yams.

At the checkout counter she wondered who the heck is Bill Thompson?

• • •

Planting trees was brutal work. The blisters on Grace's hands stung for weeks and her clothes only got dry on Sundays when everyone drove fifty miles to the nearest town just to line up for a washer and dryer at the Misty Ridge Laundromat.

At the site there were bunk houses – one for the men and one for the women, a cook house and an infirmary. David and Grace set up their own tent so that they could be together. They had a blow up air mattress and a can of sterno they used for heating up water to make the chicory drink that kept them warm on cold nights. Life was good.

One night someone gave them magic mushrooms. After a while Grace was sure she saw herself walking through the woods bare-naked but she knew she was sitting by the bonfire. David went over to take a piss up against a tree when Grace saw herself again but this time she was calling out in a taunting voice, you can't catch me.

Grace followed herself into the woods. The light of the full moon cast eerie shadows onto the trees. Faces of gnomes with elongated ears, laughing devils with red eyes and grotesque monsters with dangling tongues came at her from every direction.

After they found Grace, they took her to the infirmary where she didn't get out of bed for three days. David said he was sorry, he didn't know that anything like this would happen.

Grace smiled. "Me too," she said, "me too."

7

INVENTORY. GRACE UNDERLINED the word. Every significant item in her house would go to someone or to some place. The treadle sewing machine would go to her sister, the four poster pine bed to her friend Sylvia who came down once a year from her sheep farm. She loved that bed. Every time she stayed over she'd say it was the best night's sleep she'd ever had. And the maple dining room set would go to her cousin's twenty year old daughter Phoebe who just had a baby girl and was raising the child on her own.

The rest of the furniture would go to an auction house and the proceeds would go to the local Green Party. As for her paintings - Faye could decide what to do with them.

There was only one that she wanted to give away. It was a huge painting of two ravens sitting on the shoulders of a grey bearded man clothed in fishing nets. She had painted him standing at the end of a dock with an endless body of water reaching out toward the horizon. His back is turned to the onlooker as if to say, I know you're there.

On Tuesday she'd ship the painting out west to the library on the Queen Charlottes but address it to Haida Gwaii, the most recent name used by everyone except the locals. She'd send it with a note saying that it was donated in memory of David Owens. Later she'd drop off the amendments to her will at the lawyers - just to make sure everything was "legal-beagle" as her sister would say.

• • •

By the end of September the tent was rolled up and all of their worldly possessions were neatly stashed into the front trunk of the VW. Tree planting season was done and it was time to do something else, to go somewhere else, to move on.

Some folks were going to stay for the winter in the town with the laundromat because they met someone or, as Grace joked, so they can have clean clothes.

But that autumn Grace and David went where the roads took them and by the beginning of the first snowfall they landed at mile zero of the Alaska Highway, Dawson Creek. Grace picked up a waitressing job at the Mile Zero Diner and David lucked out as an apprentice to a cabinet maker.

On Saturday nights, when her shift was over, Chuck, the owner said that Grace and David could eat all the BBQ wings they wanted. They watched Hockey Night in Canada on the television above the bar and then on Sunday they made love all day long when there wasn't much else to do in a town that rolled up its street for the Sunday-go-to-church folks.

• • •

That afternoon while the yams were boiling Grace put yellow sticky notes on the back of the family pictures - Nanny Nellie (nee Boyd) and Pappie Sean Ferguson, 1917, Alexandria town hall; great grandmother Abigail Boyd, Nellie Boyd, Lillian Ferguson and baby Faye, train station, Ottawa 1949.

Suddenly, the smell of something like burning charcoal triggered the fire alarm. The yams. Not the yams. Grace pulled the pot of charred yams off the stove and threw it into the sink. She grabbed the tea towel and waved the smoke away from the fire alarm. When that didn't work she threw open the doors and windows and the irritating squeal of disaster finally came to an end.

And so did Grace's day. Doing one simple chore was about all she could handle. The fatigue was such that even going to bed didn't make it go away. And right about now all she wanted to do was lay down on a bed of fallen leaves.

• • •

By the following spring Grace and David had saved enough money to see them through the summer and then some, so when they landed on the Queen Charlottes, they had enough money left over to buy the lumber they needed for their house on Hippie Hill and to pick up a few bits of furniture, pots and pans, dishes and cutlery, and odds and sods from the junk man who kept it all in an old garage at the side of the highway.

On Hippie Hill the world kept on spinning. On Hippie Hill Grace and David still made love most nights and then for her birthday in May, David bought her a set of oils, some brushes, an easel and three canvas frames that he made himself.

"Go for it," he said. "You can do it."

• • •

"You're coming, aren't you?" It was 8:30 in the morning. Faye had called at the ungodly hour of 8:30 to see if Grace was up for going to church.

"You go ahead without me."

Grace was still in her nightgown. The idea of going to church with Faye, Kent and her three socially dysfunctional children was not her idea of a happy-go-lucky outing. She'd have to see them on Monday anyway. She'd do her familial obligations then.

"What's the matter Grace? Are you not up to it?"

"Well, I had a rough day yesterday." Grace was thinking of the burned pot of yams but she wasn't going to tell Faye. Besides she was able to salvage enough to mix up with the pineapple and pecans. It tasted fine. "Go ahead without me."

"Are you sure?"

"I'm sure."

"You're okay"

No Faye, I'm not okay. I'm dying remember. It was a good thing Grace didn't always speak her mind.

"I'm fine."

• • •

At Art College Grace had only taken one class in oils. But what little technique she had picked up came back to her right away and it wasn't long before she had enough paintings of seascapes and local scenes to put them up at the Dogwood Café.

"These aren't half bad." A man sitting behind Grace was telling the waitress what he thought of her work. "Bold colors. Strong stroke. By a woman? Not bad."

Grace wheeled around. "What do you mean not bad for a woman?"

"It's just that women usually do sweet little water colors of daisies and roses. Know what I mean. This stuff is strong. Whoever did them has talent."

"Well you're looking at her." The waitress pointed to Grace and clumsily set a plate of red snapper on his tourism placemat.

The man invited Grace to join him, said he was an art dealer from Ontario who had come out to see what he could find in the way of Haida jewelry. Grace told him who had the best deals for the best work and where to find them.

For an hour or more they talked about art, about who was hot in Toronto, about Bruegel and Rodin, about abstract versus realism. For that, the man offered to pay for her lemon meringue pie and tea, as long as she didn't mind. Grace accepted.

On their way out past the cash register he said, "I'll take the one of the fishing ships in the harbor and he wrote her a check for four hundred dollars." She had it listed at two fifty. Then he handed her his card: Jason Stoneway, Northern Impressions Gallery, Yorkville.

If you ever come out east, look me up.

8

GRACE HUNG UP the phone. Tired and frustrated. It took so much emotional energy just to reassure Faye over and over again that everything was fine. Everything was as fine as it was going to be. Grace sat on the side of her bed looking down at the brocade slippers she bought in Chinatown the last time she made it to Toronto. Good old Kensington Market, always changing, always the same – the Portuguese fish market, the barrels of Jamaican dry goods lined up on the sidewalk, the wizened Italian men sipping strong espresso in the front of the billiard hall.

Grace thought for a brief moment about how back in the '70s she had rented a garret on the third floor of an old brick house. It was right on Kensington Avenue above a cheese shop run by a Polish man who was always eager to give you samples of brie, gouda and blue cheese. It was there in that third floor flat that she and David curled up like spoons on her single bed. They didn't need an alarm thanks to the car horns honking at pedestrians and the outdoor stereo playing Polish polkas that woke them up every day except Sunday.

And on this beautiful morning the sunlight shone golden and orange through Grace's bedroom window. Particles of dust swirled effortlessly on the light rays. Grace took a huge breath as if somehow David's ashes might still be floating in the air and she could take him deep within and they'd be there in Kensington just one more night so very long ago.

• • •

One night David had stayed over at Grace's place on Kensington. In the morning he stood at the end of the bed looking down at Grace. "Let's go for a walk. Let's head down to the ferry and spend the day on the island."

Grace slowly rolled over. "Yes, let's."

That morning David made her breakfast – avocado and bananas on cornflakes with sweet whole milk. Grace had never tasted, let alone seen an avocado back in her hometown. Down on Kensington they picked up a hunk of cheese, fresh baked bread from the Jewish deli, some apples from the Korean fruit vendor and a bottle of cheap wine.

The ride on the ferry was another first for Grace. There were a lot of firsts with David it seemed. Arm in arm they stood on the front deck, the wind blowing their long hair over their faces. Grace could feel the sweet tang of freedom race over her. And on this day the certainty of their love for one another, like a fertile seed, found rich soil and began to flourish.

• • •

The sunlight beckoned Grace to go out. She put on her Ecuadorian poncho, the one she had picked up at the Anglican Church rummage sale in the spring. She grabbed her keys from the ceramic bowl on the walnut table beside the door and stepped out into the freshness of the day. The previous night's wind and rain had caused the leaves to fall. Grace walked along the damp sidewalks. The maple leaves looked like soggy cornflakes. The morning sun warmed her poncho and her purple beret as she walked toward the river. Grace made her way to the corner of the intersection, and even though there was hardly any traffic, she waited for the light to turn green before crossing. She noticed an old elm that had somehow escaped the Dutch elm disease of the 1960's. It stood majestically on the far side of the park. Several black squirrels raced with the grey ones competing for the peanuts being tossed by an older gentleman sitting on the park bench below the aging elm.

All things come from the light and all things go back to the light, she chanted to herself over and over to the slow rhythm of her steps.

• • •

That week a friend of David's loaned them a canoe and they took it out on the Humber River. Mallards, seagulls and herons were everywhere. They paddled until the sun shone crimson on the western horizon. Just as they were coming to the shore a huge owl swooped over their heads. Athena thought Grace. Goddess of wisdom.

In the evening they made a last minute decision to go and hear Pink Floyd at Maple Leaf Gardens. The lineup was huge but they managed to score some seats in the nosebleed section.

"How many people are here?" Grace was overwhelmed by the smoke, the lights, the sounds.

"About twenty thousand give or take." David said it as if this was normal.

"No," said Grace. "My hometown could fit in here three times. Really, David? Really?"

He took her head in his hands and kissed her forehead.

A few days later they were packed and heading out of the city in David's VW bug. The drive seemed to go on forever – past the office towers and construction sites, past shops and boutiques, past hundreds of intersections and sprawling suburbs, until at last they got to the farm lands.

David knew some people living on a commune just outside of Kleinberg. They could sleep on the couch that night before going out west. But first he had something he wanted to show Grace. He veered *into a long winding driveway past a row of manicured trees to a parking lot beside a log cabin.*

"This is Tom Thompson's cabin. We're at the McMichael Gallery."

Grace squealed with delight not unlike the time when she got her first watercolor set for Christmas back in '58.

They spent the whole day looking at the Group of Seven. Grace stood in front of a huge oil painting by Emily Carr. Towering evergreen trees spiraled up into the Hand of God sky. She started to shake and tears of joy welled up in the corner of her eyes. Every cell of her being was filled with ecstasy.

"That's where we're going." David put his arm around her waist. "We'll go there one day, I promise."

"I'm there already David. I'm already there."

• • •

Grace sat down on the bench to catch her breath. She turned her face toward the river. A huge freight liner heading back to the ocean appeared out of the mist between the islands. A silver haze lay like a blanket on the river and the water was as smooth as glass. The prow of the ship pushed back the water in large cresting slow motion waves.

Waves of thankfulness washed over Grace. She was thankful for this fleeting moment, for her senses which still worked some days, for the planet, for the journey she had been given, for the decision she had made. She offered up a prayer:

Just because you have given me the strength to die sooner than later, don't cause undo pain or guilt for my sister. Lord knows she feels guilty enough about things out of her control. Keep her wise and Lord, kick her kids out of the house, please send them away. And do me a favor, God, get rid of Kent. He's a bully.

• • •

Thirteen people lived in the communal house where Grace and David crashed. It had been built in the late eighteen hundreds but with the city sprawl, farmers were selling off their land like there was no tomorrow. University dropouts with a dream of 'live for today' found each other and moved in and out of the rental property. While smoking themselves into oblivion they found an escape from their parent's middle class values.

That night there must have been fifty or more people, all standing around the kitchen and the living room drinking beer, wine, tequila, vodka. When someone puked in the kitchen sink at three in the morning, people started to leave.

By noon the next day when Grace and David groaned that they were awake, Grace said she'd had a good time as far as she could remember. David looked at her bleary eyed.

"Let's go," he mumbled. "Let's get out of here."

Truth was Grace was glad they were leaving. Too much of a bad thing could get addictive.

• • •

At her last visit the doctor gave Grace a prescription for morphine. The cancer had spread throughout her whole body. It was taking root and it wasn't going to give in to drought, flood or chemotherapy. Sometimes the morphine made the nausea worse. Sometimes it made her feel a heavenly bliss. It lifted her higher than the trees, higher than the hills, higher than the clouds. Sometimes she was woman in the moon.

9

THE MAIL FELL to the floor through the slot in the front door. Grace made a mental note that she hoped would stay put - must cancel all mail. She rifled through the collection of junk mail - fliers for weed removal, an investment seminar, discounts at the More For Less store - then a letter with the return address for PCI - her old high school.

High School was mostly forgettable like a lot of things these days. The majority of her high school years had been washed away when she moved out of town back in '69. Gone were the names and faces of the football team and the cheerleaders who showed off their underwear doing cartwheels on the sidelines.

Only when the radio played a flashback hit like Jimmie Hendrix or Bob Dylan, only then did Grace remember the afternoons with Terry necking in the shade of the oak tree back behind the barn, and the intense heat that rose up between her legs.

• • •

In health class, Miss Ripley, who had never been married, gave the girls a lecture on how the millions of polliwog shaped sperm fought their way up the fallopian tubes toward the ovary. But only one little fellow would make it to the prized egg. And it had to be at the right moment, at that precise time of ovulation and "whamo your preggers" – at least that's how the girls in the change room described it after gym class.

Hand jobs won't get you pregnant. That was Cheryl's philosophy and from the hickies on her neck, Grace knew that she knew what she was talking about.

In the darkness of the gym while slow dancing to "Blue Velvet" Terry felt Grace up and down and held her so close she could feel him getting hard up against her leg. They decided to go steady and only explore each other and no one else.

Each time when the heavy petting grew stronger Grace would suddenly remember that she really wanted to be a good girl, to please her parents if not, herself. And in the middle of a long French kiss, Miss Ripley's voice would come up in her head – it only takes one time to get pregnant.

• • •

Grace threw the invitation to the fiftieth high school reunion into the recycling basket under the sink. No point she thought. She'd already said her good-byes to those who really mattered in her life – Sylvia on the farm, Jonathon in the city. They didn't know that it was a farewell visit but Grace did and she replayed every moment of those visits like a slide show in her brain.

Her brain was making her do stupid things. She'd taken all of her house plants to the back yard and dumped them in the composter. Faye thought that Grace was trying to make life simpler. But then a few days later Grace tried to water the dried flower arrangement on her coffee table.

When the water trickled all over the mahogany Grace burst into gales of laughter. All she could do was laugh and laugh and laugh. It was the best laugh she'd had since they told her that the treatments had come to an end and so would she one day. What else was she to do? Cry?

• • •

Terry said they had to end it. He'd had enough. And he gave Grace back the pumpkin seed necklace she'd made him for Christmas. He chose to do it in the cafeteria with everyone chowing down hot dogs and chilly for lunch.

On the way home that afternoon Grace walked by the cheap motel on the outskirts of town – the same motel she walked by twice a day, every day on her way to and from school. Some of the boys said there was a girl who'd do it for cheap over there but Grace figured it was just boy bragging lies.

That's when Grace saw him at the back of the motel. Her father. He was leaning against his Buick and he was kissing a woman in a blue mini dress.

"Dad?"

"Jesus."

At that moment Grace's fairytale world came tumbling down like shattered glass on a hardwood floor.

• • •

Grace grabbed the broom from the broom closet and began sweeping up the shards of broken glass. Another one bites the dust, she thought. It seemed that every day something fell out of her hands, something got smashed in the sink, and this morning if she was lucky maybe she wouldn't walk into any walls.

The black eye she got last week became a bit of a joke. She told the Post Office clerk that she got it pole vaulting. At the drug store she told the pharmacist that she picked up a real winner at Shooters

Billiard Bar on the weekend. She might be losing her muscle control but at least she wasn't losing her sense of humor.

Grace wiped up the mess with a worn out dish rag. She carefully used both hands to carry her mug over to the computer that she'd left on by mistake. Grace typed in 'death by exposure' and a slew of sites popped up on the screen.

Dying from exposure to cockroaches – too CSI thought Grace. Scroll.

Dying from exposure to smoke – No thanks. Scroll.

Dying from exposure to flames.

Grace thought about the story of the guy who died from spontaneous combustion. All that was left were his shoes and his charred remains in the winged-back chair in front of the television that was still on a week later. Gross.

Scroll.

You've got to be kidding. Alligators. Forget that. Scroll.

And then she saw her way out. It would do perfectly.

• • •

Grace did not tell her mother about her father's indiscretion. She buried the pain somewhere between her bowels and her bladder. For a week she was constipated followed by a urinary tract infection that the Cranberry juice did not cure.

Her mother set up an appointment with the doctor. He gave Grace a prescription for an antibiotic and a packet of birth control pills.

One Sunday night, it was shortly after the Ed Sullivan show, Grace called Terry and said she'd been thinking things over. She would. She would meet him Monday after school in their usual secret place behind the barn.

The week after Terry moved away Grace got her period. Never in her life had she been so relieved to have such pain.

10

GRACE SMILED. THIS autumn the squirrels were going absolutely bonkers – chattering at each other, flicking their tails in the air, stuffing their mouths with nuts. Grace watched them through the window above her dining room table. She scanned her immediate universe – the row of hostas, the Japanese maple, the spruce hedge. In the corner of the window a spider web swayed in the gentle breeze and the autumn sun shimmered like tinsel on the morning frost that in the early hours had joyfully painted the back yard in a silvery white hue.

Just then a monarch butterfly landed on the hummingbird feeder that Grace had been meaning to bring inside. Grace mused about how scientists were completely baffled by the instinct, the knowing, and the power of the monarch to migrate thousands and thousands of miles, riding the air currents all the way to a tree somewhere in Mexico. Millions of wings fluttering millions of times. Life was amazing.

• • •

Grace hung up the phone and ran around the house on Hippie Hill to David's woodworking shed.

"The library called. They want to show my work. Can you believe it David? I'm going to have an exhibition." Grace swirled three hundred and sixty degrees and threw herself into David's arms.

David said that this was great news, but his face told Grace another story.

"What's up, David?" Grace was baffled. "I thought you'd be happy for me. I've been working toward this for five years."

David set his wood carving tools down beside the bowl he was making.

"You're jealous."

"No, it's not that. It's not that at all."

Grace was beginning to feel her insecurities rise up in anger. "Then what is it, for crying out loud. I thought you'd be happy for me."

"I am happy for you Grace. It's something else."

Grace stared, hands on her hips.

"It's the logging. There's this company from back east. They've already ruined the northern islands, now they're threatening to clear cut some of the islands further south. They're going to ruin everything here – the whole environment will be gone – wiped out. They've got to be stopped Grace. This can't happen here. It can't."

Grace had never seen David so upset. His teeth were clenched and his eyes were moist with tears of rage.

"Jesus, David we've got to do something."

• • •

She couldn't put it off any longer. It was already four o'clock and if she didn't go over to Faye and Kent's, who knows, they might call 911 like they did when she went to the dentist and forgot to tell Faye she was going to be out. Grace appreciated her sister's concern but sometimes a little breathing room would be nice while she still had time to breathe.

The taxi company dispatcher said they'd be there in ten minutes.

Grace looked at the Georgia O'Keefe calendar on the back of the basement door. Thanksgiving Monday - yam casserole. Tuesday - ship out parcels. Wednesday - laundry. Thursday - pack. Friday - leave.

Grace slid the print out of the Willow Tree Resort into her purse, along with her meds and her lipstick. She had her plan memorized – I'm going away for five days. This may be my last chance. Don't worry. I'll be fine. Yes, they will pick me up at the bus station. Yes, there's a hospital in the town. No, I won't go swimming in the pool if no one's there.

The cab driver leaned on his horn.

Jeez, no way that was ten minutes.

It was only when she was half way to the cab that she remembered the yam casserole. Damn those yams anyway. And she left without them.

• • •

After piling up the dishes from the fish stew that David made for supper, Grace and David sat down by the light of the coal oil lantern to talk about the clear cutting.

"There's a bunch of the guys going to head up north on Sunday. We're going to camp on the land that's under dispute." David rubbed his hands on his denim jeans. "We'll stay as long as it takes. Go in rotation. Three days up and three days back. We'll go all damn summer if we have to."

Grace was quiet for a long time then she whispered, "Thuja plicata."

"Thuja what?"

"Thuja plicata – it's Latin for the Western Red Cedar."

"And?"

"And, that's what I want to call the exhibition. David, you know how I've been painting trees and the mystical aspect of... well you know what I mean. We'll call it Thuja Plicata –

Spirits of the Western Rain Forests. And I'll donate fifty percent of my sales to protecting our forests."

"If the librarian will go for it."

"Leave that with me."

• • •

"You left it behind? But Grace we love your yam casserole. Oh never mind, never mind we've got plenty to eat, plenty. Damn it who took the cork screw? Somebody find the cork screw."

For Faye making a meal for a holiday was always predictable chaos and she had a knack of getting herself as wound up as a cat in a ball of barbed wire.

"I've got it." Jackson crooned affectedly. He sauntered out of his room, with the corkscrew in his hands.

Faye put a huge emphasis on the word, what. "What was it doing in your room? You're only sixteen, never mind, hand me that. Angela, stir the gravy."

Angela silently obeyed. This was not unusual for Angela who never said anything to the point of being pathologically shy or rude. She rolled her eyes and did as she was told.

Meanwhile Steven, the sadist, was outside teasing the dog into a frenzy of barking hysterics.

"Shut up!" Kent bellowed from his easy boy chair lodged front and centre with the football game on the oversized television that swallowed up a third of the back room.

Grace escaped to the immaculate living room and sat in the rocker next to Faye's china cupboard. It was full of figurines and one too many crystal wedding gifts that were never used, not even at Christmas.

The rocking motion of the chair made her nauseous and so did her sister's family.

11

GRACE WONDERED IF she'd get resistance from Tanya, the local librarian. Her father was from the mainland and her mother was the daughter of a Haida chief. There had been plenty of people in the Haida community who thought that the logging was a good thing. It made work and it was their land after all; they could do what they wanted with it.

They met at the Dogwood Café. Grace explained her point of view. The clear cutting would destroy the Western Red Cedar and the Sitka Spruce, the whole habitat would be affected. The deer and the birds would disappear.

"We live in wood houses." Tanya sounded pragmatic.

"It's what we have here. If we had brick we'd use brick," Grace argued. "And besides we aren't selling the wood we have to some huge hardware store south of the border or helping to build houses in the California desert."

"And that husband of yours he uses wood to make bowls."

"We're not married. It's found pieces that he collects off the ground and from the beach."

"What about the fires in our wood stoves?"

"I know, I know. We should go solar but you just try that in a rainforest."

Tanya laughed. "I'm just giving you a hard time. Of course you can use your proceeds any way you want."

"And the posters? We can promote the cause on the posters?"

"Yes. Are you going to use paper? Paper comes from trees you know." Tanya had a wicked sense of humor. And Grace liked her for it.

• • •

The one thing lacking around these so called festive occasions at Faye's house was the festivity. Everyone was so damn serious. And pious. Kent always said a blessing over the meal even though he hadn't set foot inside a church since Angela was baptized. Everyone bowed their heads in solemn sublimation or avoidance to his patriarchal authority.

Grace kept her mouth shut about what she was really thinking although lately she had been telling complete strangers what was on her mind. Like last week when someone at the movies left their cell phone on Grace yelled, you'll get a tumor on your brain if you use that thing. And then it hit her – what she had said.

Over dinner Grace made a feeble attempt to engage Angela in a conversation.

"How's school?"

"Fine."

"And your grades? How are they going?"

"Fine."

"What's your favorite subject?"

Shrug.

Jackson sported a circular ear ring that made a hole the size of a dime in his left lobe. Grace thought she'd have better luck talking with him.

"What's new with you buster?' Grace had always called him buster on account he was born with a full crop of brown hair – thus Buster Brown.

Jackson bragged on about his skateboarding, his guitar lessons, his new girl friend, his tattoo on his back.

Grace was drifting off to some long ago time when she heard Kent bellow, "Tattoo."

The dinner crisis had begun. It never failed; there'd always be one.

• • •

David grabbed Grace by the arm and took her to the alcove between the men's and women's washrooms at the library gallery. He slipped his hands under her blouse, felt her bare breast and kissed her neck, her cheek, her lips.

"Hey you, someone's going to see us."

"Let them."

"Look, I've got to get back and be the hostess. This is my opening silly. I need to make sure that there's enough smoked salmon and besides, the guy pouring the wine seems to be helping himself just a little too much."

"Alright then Miss Artiste, you do what you have to do and I'll see you in three days time. I'm heading up with the gang tonight."

"Tonight?"

"The guys figure we'll get there in the pitch back, make a nice little surprise for the crew when they show up in the morning. We've got a CBC television team on board. We're all set."

And he kissed Grace one last time.

• • •

After the tattoo crisis passed and Steven asked to be excused early so he could meet up with his friends who were going to watch the last of the game at someone else's house, Faye brought up the inevitable.

"You know Grace, I don't think it's such a good idea, you going away on your own right now, with the spells you've been having and you know, it just wouldn't be a good idea…"

"For Christ sake Faye, let her do whatever the hell she wants." Kent put in his own inebriated two cents.

Faye clammed up and started clearing the table in a furry not unlike the squirrels in Grace's backyard. For the one and only time in her life, Grace was thankful that Kent was a bully.

• • •

It was midnight. Grace walked through the light drizzle back to her home on the hill. She could see that David had left the lights on for her, something they never did for themselves. The emptiness of the bed made it impossible for Grace to fall sleep, that combined with all the verbal muddle crashing about her brain after the gala. The next night was no better. Whenever David went away fishing or to see a friend on the mainland Grace was completely sleep deprived until his return when she would sleep for twelve hours straight after they made love.

On the third night she decided to wear his sweatshirt to bed but that didn't help either. She would be restless until he was in her arms again.

• • •

Grace offered to help with the clean up but Faye insisted that she could manage, that Grace looked like death warmed over.

"Oh, my God, Grace I didn't mean – it's just – oh."

• • •

It was sometime around eight at night on the fourth day that the cruiser pulled up in front of their house on Hippie Hill. They said that David had been driving his motorcycle south on the coastal road. He'd gone off an embankment and hit a tree. He died instantly.

Suddenly all time and meaning vanished from the earth. Grace fell to her knees and screamed out his name - screamed out his name into the purple depths of the last of the light of day.

II

A few minutes ago every tree was excited, bowing to the roaring storm, waving, swirling, tossing their branches in glorious enthusiasm like worship. But though to the outer ear these trees are now silent, their songs never cease.

~John Muir

12

DURING THE WAKE, all Grace could feel was numb. So many people had come out to the community hall to celebrate David's life. So many people loved David, for his generosity, for his passion, for his devil-may-care enthusiasm. And Grace's love for David was greater than anything imaginable.

Local musicians played until midnight, all the songs that David used to sing when he jammed with his friends – 'any day now, any day now, I shall be released'. People embraced Grace. They cried and she stood there, the strong one, the brave one, the numbness taking her further and further away.

At night Grace lay in their bed in their empty house on Hippie Hill staring up at the ceiling. She could feel him slipping away from her – the thread from her heart to his being pulled tighter and tighter with each breath. Grace curled up on her side and hugged the pillow where David would have rested his head if he had come home. She knew she had to let him go, but God, why so soon? Why?

• • •

The clock said 5:30 and for a moment Grace wasn't sure if it was in the morning or in the evening; she had been sleeping so much these past few weeks. She grabbed the remote on the bed stand and flicked on the television to the weather network. The reporter said that it would be seasonal temperatures all day – they were calling for a bright, crisp autumn morning to get you up and off to work.

Grace did not feel bright and crisp - if anything she felt dull and sluggish. She sat on the side of her bed and prepared to stand up. Slowly, she coached herself. Last week when she stood up after having a nap she had fallen over, taking the nightstand, the lamp, and her glass of water with her. Just being was becoming a chore in itself.

• • •

It was a strange ritual – bringing someone food to feed the body when the soul was starving. Grace stared at the pile of leftovers in her fridge. She realized that after three weeks of collecting mould it was time to throw out the baked lentils and vegetarian lasagna that her friends had brought around after the funeral. She closed the door, leaned her forehead against the cold metal and listened to the hum of its motor. Later - she'd deal with it all later.

Eating seemed somehow unnecessary and Grace took to painting for hours on end, only getting up to pour another coffee or to head out to the squatter for a pee.

The oils on her canvas became intense. Broad strokes broke away from the predictable flow of landscapes. They danced in a fierce and violent dimension that surprised even Grace. Blood red swashes of paint dissected yellow swirls and streaks of black and green raced at right angles.

There were moments when Grace was not in control of her strokes. Once she closed her eyes and let the energy travel from her heart to her hand and it was beautiful – a blue wave-like ribbon floated onto the open canvas.

• • •

Damn it. Damn it to hell. Faye would not find out about this.

Grace had managed to come to a standing position but as soon as she tried to move her left foot it stayed put and she nearly fell into the door. Her head ached as if it were being squeezed in a giant vice grip.

Still trembling, Grace sat on the side of her bed and reached for the plastic container on the night stand. Fumbling with the cap she shook two morphine pills into her hands, swallowed them and waited for that moment of bliss.

In a little while she would try again to make it to the shower but for now she'd sit up in bed and watch a little of the early morning shows – how to make butter tarts, switch, the threat of a flu-like pandemic in South America, switch, buy milk, switch, and in the middle east....Grace nodded off... switch.

• • •

Friends offered to come over and help Grace clean up David's workshop, but Grace said, not right now - maybe later. Everything could be later, couldn't it? Like washing the dishes or doing laundry. It could wait, couldn't it?

Her friends called her on the phone.

I'm really tied up, you know. I'm busy painting. No, don't come over. No, I can't go to the picnic on Friday, I'm painting. Yeah, that's right there's a lot to do after a funeral. Okay, so like, I've got to go now. Bye.

At first her friends reached out. They'd come to the door but Grace would only open it a crack and she'd say she was too tired or too busy of too something and eventually they stopped calling altogether.

But Grace was never alone. She could feel David beside her as she painted. She could smell the sweet cent of cedar on the wind as he brushed past her and once she was sure she heard him call her name. He stayed beside her for well over a month and at night she dreamed dreams of flying, the two of them holding hands and rising higher and higher above the trees toward the luminous night sky.

13

THE JARRING RING of the phone startled Grace out of her dreams and back into reality. It was Faye making her daily check in call.

The usual. "How are you? Oh, did I wake you up?"

"No, I was just having a little rest. What time is it?"

"Noon."

"Right - noon."

"Are we still on for tea at two?" Faye sounded hesitant. "At the Windmill Café?"

Grace had forgotten, and she hadn't been out of bed, or had her shower, or checked her calendar to see what day of the week it was, and everything was swirling like cows in a tornado.

"Jesus, Faye, how can you be hungry after that huge feast you made yesterday?" Grace snapped.

"It's just that, I thought you wanted to, never mind, we'll do it next week."

"Next week – I'm going away – remember?"

"I don't think you should go Grace, I really don't think…"

"Pick me up at two. I'll be ready."

After they hung up Grace stared at the blank wall - stunned. She needed to say good-bye to Faye – to see her for the last time. And for a very brief moment she wondered if she was doing the right thing.

• • •

The last time David made a dream visit to Grace there was huge storm blowing in from the Pacific. Torrents of rain whipped against the window panes and Grace thought for sure the gales would blow the house all the way down Hippie Hill and out to sea.

Grace cocooned herself in David's old sleeping bag and rocked herself in and out of sleep. All night Grace tossed about on the bed not unlike a ship on the ocean until finally, she fell asleep from sheer exhaustion.

By morning the storm had subsided and a shimmering mist hung on the branches of the trees outside the bedroom window. Unconsciously Grace threw open the sleeping bag and turned over to lay spread-eagle on her back.

Her energy rose up half way out of her body. She was sitting up and yet she could see her upper body lying motionless below her. Then she sailed out completely and stood at the end of the bed watching. Suddenly in a way that no words would ever describe Grace knew David had entered into her body. He was one within her being. And in a heart-wrenching cry of the longest imaginable sorrow Grace awoke and David was gone - forever.

• • •

Faye stood in the living room examining a neatness that she had rarely seen in her sister's house.

"Place looks great Grace. It's so feng shui."

"About time don't you think?" Grace was determined to put on her best attitude and her best hat for this, the last time that she would be with Faye.

"You're limping". Faye didn't need to be a rocket scientist to see that Grace was dragging her left foot. You've had a stroke for Christ sake.

"Don't be ridiculous. You're such an alarmist. I strained it putting out the recycling this morning. It's nothing." Grace offered a little white lie.

"We should have it looked at."

"No we shouldn't. Come on I'm starving." Another untruth.

Grace was never very hungry these days but Faye, who had battled her weight since she was twelve, could never resist an opportunity to eat out. Grace dangled the temptation as a form of distraction.

"You're sure you're okay."

"Yes, yes, yes, a thousand times yes. Faye, let's not talk about me today. Let's talk about anything else, okay. Let's have a nice lunch out, just the two of us." And Grace thought to herself, we can even talk about your kids if you insist, anything, but not about how sick I am.

• • •

Grace didn't get dressed at all that day after David's dream visit. She shuffled her feet inside her moccasins, walking around and around in circles – over to the wood stove – over to her paintings – over to the sofa – over to the sink.

Grace sauntered over to the closet and pulled out David's leather motorcycle jacket and smelled the arm pits for the scent of the musk that he put on his body. It lingered in her nostrils and she called out his name, she called so loud that the ravens called back. But David he did not come to her that day or the next or the day after that. He was gone. David was gone.

• • •

The orange ginger soup stared up at Grace. It had always been on her top list of choices at the Windmill Café but today it seemed to be too bitter and too strong for her waning appetite. Faye kept telling Grace to eat more, to just try a little more and to appease her sister Grace dutifully took a little taste and then put the spoon down.

Grace told Faye what a wonderful sister she was – how there would have been no way she could have gone through the treatments on her own. And she thanked Faye for being there when Grace broke her arm trying to do the balance beam walk across the top of the teeter-totters in the park. And for the time Faye lied to her parents about Grace being at the bowling alley when she had gone necking with Terry in his father's car.

They laughed like they hadn't laughed in years and for a brief moment Faye got to stop worrying about Grace, about her creep of a husband and her three spoiled kids. Faye got to be the girl she'd once been until the day she married Kent when she had just turned nineteen and she was three months pregnant.

And for the lunch she did not eat and this moment of true happiness she saw glowing within Faye's eyes, Grace was thankful.

• • •

Grace looked at the mess she had been living in for God knows how long. And she looked at her face in the mirror, her cheek bones more prominent than ever before, her red hair matted and unkempt.

My God, thought Grace, if David were here he'd have a bird. He'd friggin' freak out. She shoved a pile of the Island Reporter newspapers off the worn out wicker chair and sat down with her sudden awareness that nearly two months had passed since the funeral.

It was time. Time to get back to the land of the living. Time to move on. But where? Her whole life for the past five years had been rooted on these islands but somehow none of that resonated any more. David was gone and so were her reasons for staying.

Grace looked at the chaos and the disarray that she had not really noticed was encroaching on her ethereal existence for these past several weeks. She walked over to her desk thinking this was as good a place to start as any. The rubble of pots and pans and dishes in the sink and on the counter could wait.

The desk was littered with scum filled coffee mugs, half eaten sandwiches, an empty beer bottle, stacks of unopened mail, newspapers, receipts, a pizza box, a stack of books.

Grace pulled out a book of poems once spun by the mystic Rumi seven centuries ago. It fell open to a page that was marked with a business card – Jason Stoneway, Northern Impressions Gallery, Yorkville.

Turn from the ocean now

Toward dry land

Grace looked at the stack of her paintings leaning against the living room wall. She would call the gallery in the morning.

14

JASON SAID OF course he remembered who she was and how she had led him to some of the best silver pieces he had found anywhere on of the entire west coast.

"I'm looking at your painting as we speak. I put it in my office. So what is the pleasure of your call this fine day may I ask."

Grace suddenly felt a knot in her stomach that cried out, you stupid fool he just wants to get you into his bed.

"Well, it's just that, you see, I've really changed my style lately and I thought maybe I could send you a portfolio or something and besides I'm thinking of moving back to Toronto, except that I don't have a place to stay and well, you're probably busy now, maybe I should call back." Grace felt like she was in first grade all over again, making excuses for being alive.

There was silence on the other end of the line.

"Right then, I guess I shouldn't have called."

"No, no, I'm thinking. I'm thinking. Let me call you back later. I may have something of interest. What's your number?"

Grace gave Jason her number, and after they had hung up Grace kicked the footstool clear across the living room floor into the table beside her arm chair and the vase full of wild flowers spilled in slow motion onto a pile of *Heritage Living* magazines.

Crap it to hell. I'm an idiot. I should never have called.

• • •

After their lunch at the Windmill Café Faye dropped Grace off at her house just as the courier was pulling up.

"Expecting a parcel?"

"Nope."

"What then?"

"I'm sending a painting out to B.C."

"Okay then, well, take it easy. I'll call you tomorrow. Don't forget to send me the information on the resort okay. Great lunch." Faye gave Grace a hug and jumped into her car. She waved out the window. "Bye Gracie-girl."

Grace watched as Faye drove her compact grey Honda around the corner and out of sight. An ominous feeling flushed over her face.

Bye Faye. Bye. She whispered to herself. Bye. Grace knew that this day had been one of the best times they had had in a long time and it would be their last.

• • •

When David died Grace called her mother back home.

"…No, Mom, you don't need to come. I've got lots of friends out here and besides it's a long trip for you… church… ah, no Mom, we didn't go to church…oh, there's a Unitarian lay preacher, she's a friend of mine, yeah, she'll do the service.… Yes, Mom I'm sure, besides…

I think that you've got your hands full helping Faye with the new baby…what's that …no, don't send any money…for Christmas…I'll try… love you too…bye.…bye."

David's parents did come out and they stayed at a B & B in town. The house on Hippie Hill wouldn't have suited them even though Grace did offer. She wasn't really surprised that they had refused her generosity.

From everything David had told her about his parents, they lived a very upper, upper middle class existence in Thornhill. No the modest little home on Hippie Hill was a bit too rustic for the Owens.

Mr. Owens was an accountant and Shirley, Mrs. Owens, she had a job as a school secretary. Grace had only met them once before at a summer picnic north of Peterborough. Her first impression was that they were too heavily into polyester and processed cheese. Sure, they were nice enough but the luring looks that David's father gave Grace made Shirley act suspicious and gave Grace the creeps.

They offered to take David's ashes back to Ontario but Grace stood her ground.

"David belongs out here with the trees and the ocean. This place was his whole life. It meant everything to him. Everything."

Shirley came right back at Grace.. "What about those first eighteen years? What about that?" And she ran out of the community hall sobbing.

"Guess we're going now." Mr. Owens followed his wife through the double doors of the funeral home.

The next day when they left for the airport they didn't bother to go up to the house that David had built on Hippie Hill. And they didn't bother to say good-bye to Grace which was just as well since Grace was in no way capable of handling the emotional blackmail. They just disappeared like a letter lost in the mail with no return address.

• • •

Things had really changed since the seventies.

Grace held a packet of photographs that she had taken of David during their travels out west. Back then she used an old clunky Pentax with a zoom lens. Nowadays everything was digital – cameras, computers, cell phones, CDs, DVDs and for Grace it was all she could do to teach herself how to use e-mail and the internet and even that was pretty shabby at times.

Grace pulled out a picture of David standing in front of the mile zero sign post on the Alaska Highway. He had on threadbare bell bottom jeans and cowboy shirt he'd picked up in Banff. His long jet-black hair had been blown across his forehead and he looked down at the photographer with a devilish grin, his thumb held out in a hitch-hiking pose.

God you were good looking. We thought we'd live forever, didn't we? Grace put aside a few picture for herself. The rest she tucked into a brown mailer. She would send them to the Owen's. But where did they live if indeed they were still alive?

Despite her lack of computer skills it didn't take long for Grace to do a search of the internet to find the obituary for Ronald Owens. He'd passed away last June. Grace read through the funeral home listing… survived by his wife Shirley Owens of Lakefield…predeceased by his son David Andrew Owens…donations to the Alzheimer's Society.

Grace addressed the envelope to Mrs. R. Owens in care of Blakey's Funeral Home. She put in a note to please forward the photographs to the family. Grace pulled off the self sealing strip of the envelope, attached a stamp and put the kettle on for a cup of tea. She'd mail it next time she went out.

15

THE HIGH-PITCHED SQUEAL of the kettle broke into Grace's dream as if it were a factory whistle calling the men back to work in an old 1930's documentary. She'd nodded off on the couch.

Grace stood up so quickly that it seemed as if the room lurched upward tossing Grace like a rag doll on a thrill ride at the Ex. She hit her forehead on the edge of the coffee table and the next thing Grace knew she was lying on the floor looking up at the ceiling swirling above.

When she managed to pull herself together, she wondered where the little yellow canaries had gone to – the ones that usually circle around the head of the animated cat when it gets knocked out in the cartoons. Faye might think this was funny, but Faye wouldn't find out about Grace's cut on her forehead. Faye would be able to stop worrying very soon.

• • •

"Stop it Grace. Stop doing that." Grace's mother called from the kitchen.

Grace looked at the flowered linoleum on the floor of her parent's house. She was five years old and she loved making the world spin. Round and round she'd twirl until the whole room flew about in the air –

then she'd fall backwards into the safety of the old stuffed sofa and she'd watch the ceiling become the floor and the floor become the ceiling all circling around and around ever slower until they stopped. And then she'd do it again.

"Stop it I tell you. You'll hurt your brain."

• • •

Grace popped a couple of morphine capsules to ease her throbbing head. Pain management, that's what the doctor had told her. Take them before the pain gets out of control.

For once in her life Grace really felt like her life was in her own hands and that she no longer had to worry about being in or out of control. She had an ever increasing feeling of her own temporariness which seemed to disperse all vulnerability or fear. They'd vanished like dandelion seeds in the wind.

She'd stopped wondering why this was happening to her. It just was. She wasn't angry with God or David's parents or her father or anyone for that matter. Anger had no place in her heart anymore. It just wasted her energy and what little time she had left to do what she needed to do.

She'd stopped trying to analyze the things she had done in her life that might have caused the tumor to be planted in her head. She didn't worry that it might have been the hair dyes she used in her forties before turning grey was acceptable by her own standards of self worth.

It didn't matter that it could have been some sort of contamination. It had crossed her mind that breathing in the asbestos fibers dangling from the broken insulation in the attic of her parent's post war house could have posed a health risk but at that time people were more concerned that the Russians were going to drop a nuclear bomb on the school. Maybe that's why everyone had to practice hiding under their desks. Maybe that's why Kennedy was assassinated.

Then there were the summers when her father used to spray the inside the rental cottage with DDT to kill the mosquitoes. The whole family huddled in the car and waited half an hour before going back inside to open the windows. Grace still remembered that on those nights everyone easily fell asleep to the sweet smell of the toxin.

• • •

Grace knew that the Charlottes were small but she had no idea how fast the news would spread that she was moving back to that filthy, self-centered city they called "Tarana". The general attitude of the westerners was, who would want to live there, or I went there once and never again, or I have cousin in Toronto, don't know how she stands it.

But Grace was truly blown away when the guild of artisans threw a surprise bon voyage lunch at the Dogwood Café. It was Tanya's idea. She had become Grace's closest friend on the island. They'd spent a lot of time together when the "boys" were away. They'd read each other's tarot, drank copious amounts of red wine, and cried over unfulfilled passions. They were so wise and so naive and so close. It would be hard to leave Tanya behind.

We've made you a quilt. Each of us. We each made a square. It's our version of Judith Chicago without the plates.

Grace remembered recently reading about the huge exhibition where a group of women created voluptuous vaginas as a celebration of womanhood. On this quilt, made by the hands of the island women, there was one square with a naked woman embracing a salmon. Another square had a woman with the head of a raven. Interspersed were Haida images in red and black – frog woman, otter and wolf.

Tanya draped the quilt over her shoulders – to Queen Grace. Long may she paint, long may she live.

• • •

Grace repeated the words, all's well in my world, as she wandered down the hall to her bedroom. All's well in my world. All's well in my world.

And with that thought Grace slipped into a night of beautiful dreams. Dreams of star spirals swirling in a blue-black sky, then standing on the patio of an outdoor café overlooking the Mediterranean in the south of Spain, and swimming naked in a lake with David. The rise of her body to the memory of his touch filled her with ecstasy until dawn.

16

TANYA WAS THE first person that Grace had told that she was moving. They'd both gone down to the fishing docks to wait for a load of red snapper to come in. Sometimes the fishermen would give them the scrawny ones for cheap.

Grace explained that she'd met Jason a couple of years ago - that he'd bought one of her paintings. He was willing to help her get settled in Toronto.

"So where are you going to live?" Tanya asked as she tossed a stone from the beach into the ocean.

"Well, Jason called last week and he said that there is a studio loft available in the same warehouse where he lives."

"And how are you going to - you know - make a living? Toronto ain't cheap."

"He's got this gallery in Yorkville and he said I could be the receptionist for a couple days a week while I get things sorted out."

Tanya took a deep breath and then, "You're okay with this?"

Grace shrugged. "Yeah, I'm okay."

"Then, me too." Tanya embraced Grace and the salt air caressed them.

. . .

Right on schedule. Grace drew a big "X" across Tuesday on the calendar. It was Wednesday and it was laundry day even though there really wasn't much to do. Grace had gone through her chest of drawers weeks ago, weeding out the never worn, over worn, and out of fashion items. Some of the old bras went straight into the garbage - along with her tattered underpants that only God knows why she still had them.

She was the daughter of a daughter of the depression which explained the collection of rubber bands on the knob of the basement door and the jar of twist ties that she kept on the kitchen counter. Besides too much of humankind's inventions were disposable - plastic plates, tin cans, old car tires, computers.

As far as Grace was concerned all of this recycling crap was only a band-aid for the real problem – consumerism. Life should be like jazz where "less is more". The less you have the freer you become. The more you have, the greater the weight upon your earthy shoulders. And Grace was feeling lighter and lighter every day – so light she could sail away with the clouds on a windswept morning.

• • •

Flying was not high up on the list of Grace's favorite past times. She had only once before been up in an airplane, the Grey Goose that she and David took to the Queen Charlottes five and a half years ago.

To add to her anxiety, on this morning, there had been a delay in Vancouver. The airport was socked in with fog. Sitting on the chrome airport bench Grace sipped a diet cola in hopes of calming her nerves. No luck. They just got worse. Finally the call to board the plane - passengers needing assistance please proceed to gate fourteen.

Eight hours later the jet broke through a low cover of clouds that seemed to hover precariously close to the sprawling megalopolis below. Grace was sure the plane was going to miss the runway. She closed her eyes and dug her fingernails into the arm rests and prepared for the inevitable.

There was a slight bump, a bit of a jostle, followed up with the crackling voice of the stewardess over the PA, Welcome to Toronto.

• • •

Every detail of her trip was laid out on the dining room table in two piles – one for Faye and one for her true destination to a provincial park in Quebec, back of Maniwaki.

Faye had called earlier. Grace could hear the concern in her sister's voice even though she had stopped harping on about the whole idea of Grace going to a resort, especially going alone. Grace tried to keep the conversation light.

"Yes, Faye I was just about to send you an e-mail with the information about the resort. Who knows maybe you and Kent could go there sometime."

Faye told Grace that she'd had this weird dream. She said that in the dream Grace was walking through a forest toward a meadow – sort of like in a Disney movie, she said, "It was all soft focus and there was a wolf standing in the meadow. You put your arms around its neck and you know what was really weird?"

"No, What was really weird?"

"You had branches of oak leaves growing out of your hair sort of like Medusa and snakes but sort of not."

"Now that is weird."

"But you looked beautiful, Grace. You looked like you were eighteen."

"Well there you go. I'm only eighteen."

Faye asked Grace if she knew what it might mean.

"Beats me? You probably ate too much popcorn before going to bed, right? Anyway, I'm going to send the e-mail to you now. Talk to you tomorrow."

After Grace sent Faye the message via the great global brain, she thought about Faye's dream and Grace knew exactly what it meant.

• • •

Jason had mailed her directions to the loft – Take the airport express bus to the subway, get off at Dundas West, take the Junction streetcar southbound, get off at Sorenson and walk south two blocks. It's the four storey red brick building on your right, number 502. Buzz and I'll come down.

Grace still had a lot of "what ifs" built up inside her head, her stomach and her sweaty palms. She made her way into the clamor and confusion of the city and told herself to buck up, come on now, you lived here before, what's the big deal.

But what if Jason is some kind of perv like the profs at Art College? What if all he wants is a little chicke-poo to run his errands? What if her paintings get lost by the courier? What if? What If? What if she were a rabbit stunned by the headlights of an oncoming transport truck? What if?

III

We all travel the milky way together, trees and men... trees are travelers, in the ordinary sense. They make journeys, not very extensive ones, it is true: but our own little comes and goes are only little more than tree-wavings...

~John Muir

17

EXHAUSTED FROM THE flight, and nervous about what lay in store, Grace stared at the buzzer on the brick wall beside the industrial looking entrance to the warehouse. She took a breath then pushed it. A voice chimed over the cellophane sounding speaker – "You're here. We'll be right down."

Grace jiggled about while she waited, shivers running up and down her legs. She'd forgotten how damp and uncomfortable March could be in the city. Somehow the west coast dampness never felt quite as cold.

The huge glass door swung open. There, in the foyer, stood two men looking as happy as seals about to receive a fish at the aquarium.

Jason spoke. "Come in, come in. Don't just stand there. Bryan, give her some room."

"Here, let me take that." Bryan had on overly tight blue jeans and a white tee-shirt. He reached for Grace's backpack. Grace noticed that he sported a gold chain around his neck and his skin was bronze, as if he'd been lying on the beach for weeks or maybe spending too much time in a tanning salon.

"Out of the way silly." Jason waved at Bryan. "Let's give the girl a hug."

With each step that they took up the stairs to the third floor it became increasingly clear that Jason would never want to get into her *pants. He was as gay as you could get. And that pleased Grace to no end. The last thing she wanted right now was to fend of advances from members of the opposite sex.*

• • •

Grace had been meticulously thorough. Her sweaters were piled neatly in the cedar chest, her pants were all on hangers and her closet looked like something out of an ad for a trendy decorating magazine. In the top drawer of the walnut chest that her grandmother had left for her, her socks were organized by colour and length. Her life had never been so organized.

It was noon and even though Grace didn't feel like eating she knew she needed her strength to keep going, to get her to the park in Quebec. Friday would be a long day and it had been over three months since she last drove anywhere.

Grace slid open the kitchen drawer and shook the box of wax paper. The keys jingled inside. Still there. Good. She closed the drawer and opened the fridge; it was spotless.

Last week Grace had thrown out every scrap of leftovers - a smelly tuna casserole, chickpeas in a plastic container and half a can of stewed tomatoes that somehow got pushed to the back.

The tin had turned black. Grace thought about the Franklin expedition to the Arctic and how the men all went crazy when they got stranded on the ice for the second winter in a row. They'd done ridiculous things like carry a huge oak desk for hundreds of mile across the frozen tundra. All because of lead poisoning. The cans had been soldered on the inside and the lead had seeped into the food. What you don't know can kill you, thought Grace.

On the shelves of the fridge there were half empty bottles of pickles and relishes that had been given to her. Some were over ten years old. Get a life, Grace said out loud to herself, and then when she thought about the irony of what she had mumbled, it made her laugh. Out loud.

• • •

"This is your place."

Jason led the way into a huge, mostly empty loft with floor to ceiling windows all along the eastern wall. At one end, a galley kitchen had been built in, and another wall hid what was a bathroom, complete with a shower and shelving.

A 1950's vintage chrome kitchen table with a turquoise boomerang top and four mismatched chairs served as the dining area. Next to that was a well worn brown velvet couch and water stained end tables that had been left behind by the previous tenant.

Grace turned around. There they were - her paintings, still crated and leaning against the opposite wall. They'd arrived, even before she did. They were safe and so was she.

"Come on Bryan, let's give the girl a chance to do her girl thing. Dinner's at 7. We're right across the hall so you just get settled in here and we'll talk about things over dinner." Jason kissed her on the cheek and much to her surprise so did Bryan. Grace thought - what a lovely couple.

• • •

Grace decided on a banana smoothie made with protein powder, yogurt and orange juice. She took it over to the dining room table, spread open the map and with a bright yellow highlighter she began to trace her route.

She'd take the back roads. There would be fewer cops than on the major highways. Grace was not about to risk being pulled over for speeding or being stopped just because some antsy cop with an ax to grind with his ex-girlfriend suddenly decided on her shade of car. Besides if by some chance Faye got wind of Grace's plans, she'd be harder to find on the country roads.

It would take her at least two days to get there. A few years ago when Tanya had come to visit she drove them up and back in the same day. It was a long trip but she did it. Not now. She knew she'd have to take her time.

• • •

Jason poured Grace a second glass of Merlot and offered her another helping of the paella that Bryan had made for dinner. She declined politely saying this was more food than she'd eaten in years.

The conversation went from holidays on the Costa del Sol to dreadfully boring art dealers at an exhibition in New York, from the loathing of disco to summer escapades at cottages, and as the wax dripped down the sides of the burgundy candles to the base of the crooked candelabra that sat at one end of the chestnut table, Grace felt that she had somehow been adopted by two loving brothers.

After a third glass of wine Grace told them about how she and Scott had done this nudity thing when they were kids and when Bryan called her a brazen hussy the three of them laughed like school girls. By midnight they had consumed close to four bottles of wine and they had told so many life stories to each other that Grace thought that she might have even known them in a past life or maybe that was just the wine and maybe that didn't really matter if they had or had not because life was like that or was it, and what the hell, it felt good.

18

THE CHAMOMILE TEA had turned cold. Grace wondered how long she had been staring out the window. It was so easy now, to just suspend time, to hover in the moment and watch the world spin past.

There was a science program she had heard on the radio...the earth is spinning at a rate of 1000 kilometers an hour as fast as a speeding jet. And at the same time the earth is moving through space at such a rate that in a matter of a split second she could be in Toronto and in another split second she'd be back home again.

Grace felt the weight of gravity keeping her pinned to the earth when all she wanted to do was to fall off the planet, to be catapulted into space - beyond the ozone layer, beyond the solar system, beyond the galaxy, beyond the beyond.

As she glanced out the window her eyes caught the wind playing tug of war with the leaves on the red maple. It was losing more and more of its leaves every day. The gnarly old tree was a timekeeper, signaling for the birds to fly south, reminding the children to go to school, urging the farmer to bring in the harvest.

And suddenly Grace saw her cradled in the branches, Persephone, in her silken flowing gowns smiling down at Grace as if to say I know I must return to the underworld and you shall come with me.

• • •

Midmorning sunlight screamed in through the windows of the loft. Graced pulled the covers over her head and when she remembered where she was and what she was supposed to do, she heaved the covers on the floor and forced herself to sit on the edge of the bed. Grace moaned. Her head felt the size of a watermelon about to burst. Two headache pills and water. God give me water, Grace muttered as she wove her way over to the sink. So this was life in the big city. Holy crap.

Jason had said to drop by the gallery sometime in the afternoon and he would give her the lay of the land. Grace felt a churning in the pit of her stomach not unlike the feeling she had when she dropped her mittens down the hole in the school outhouse – once they were gone, they were gone for good.

And right now there was no backing out of the situation. She had a home and a job which was all good, wasn't it? It was more the fear of not knowing what kind of emotional abyss she was letting herself in for. Could she tolerate the arrogance of the upper echelon of kept wives from Forest Hill and Rosedale? Her friends on Hippie Hill would tease her about joining the ranks of the consumer driven, cash-mad Ontario elite.

Still in a fog, Grace made her way over to the bathroom sink and turned on the left facet labeled "H" for hot. The water was freezing. She tried the right faucet labeled "C" for cold and hot water came out. Go figure. Grace smiled. Life is never what you expect it be.

• • •

Hospitals were out of the question. Grace had made her mind up about that. She wasn't going to have anybody clinging to her bedside watching her deteriorate day by day, minute by minute. She'd seen enough of that when her mother died. For weeks after the internment she tried to make peace with the granite headstone, with the fresh earth piled on the grave. It didn't bring her mother back. It didn't erase the helplessness, and it didn't heal the loss.

She'd always had a plan. It was something she'd thought about off and on ever since high school when they taught the ways of the Indians as they were called back then.

Grace recalled a childhood rhyme but as she whispered it to herself it took on its own meaning - one little, two, little, three little Indians in residential schools, four little, five little six, little Indians missing or dead, seven killed by cops, eight raped and abandoned, nine protesting land claims, ten dying from mercury poisoning. Somehow the truth was never told in the history lesson plans of her high school. Life was proving to be the greater teacher.

But Grace knew of one tradition that if she had her choice she would follow. She would die in the woods. She would be like Alice Snowshoes, left to perish in the snow. Alice was old and feeble and her people, the Huron, were already scattered like seeds in the wind. They could not risk the burden of carrying the old woman with them. Grace would be a burden to no one.

• • •

The grinding wheels of the streetcar vibrated every bone in Grace's body. She had forgotten how intense the city really was. If she were a musician she would tape record all of the clangs and clatter, all of the cacophony, and blend it into a metallic orchestration.

Grace looked through the smudged streetcar windows at the stores whizzing past - Portuguese, Chinese, Vietnamese - signs for everything from electronics to a nail salons. The streetcar's wheels screeched hard against the iron rails and came to a halt at a familiar stop. It was Kensington Market - the area where she and David had danced the nights away in smoky bars, where they had bought firm avocadoes and fresh ripe mangoes, where they had explored every part of their physical, emotional, and spiritual selves. The memory that she had stored so deeply still lingered long in her body, and her sexuality was surprisingly aroused to the sweet remembrance and urged on by the rhythm of the street car.

Unexpectedly the street car lurched, just missing a man in a wheel chair. He was shaking his fist at the driver who yelled back, you idiot, you know these things can't swerve.

Grace could see the man. He was shirtless yet he bravely paddled the wheel chair with his bare feet across the six lanes of traffic. All the cars stopped. No one came to his aid. After all he was just one more little drunken Indian.

• • •

Grace surfaced slowly from her dream. She had been climbing a tree and was trying to rescue a heron that had its leg caught in fishing line. She would paint it. She would set the tree on an island on the back of turtle and the turtle would be floating in space. All manner of bird – hawk, crow, parrot, chickadee, and swan would try to release the trapped bird - and then - no – the painting days were over. They were done.

Grace felt a sudden surge of despair. In all of her logical plans for her final journey she had somehow managed to block out the sentimentality of living - of being a creative entity. It had been months since she last painted anything. And now, just as she was about to leave, she was feeling sadly inspired.

19

GRACE SPLASHED THE warm water over her breasts and the scent of the Juniper foam bath rose up from the soaker tub. She had it installed with the money from her mother's will. That was about all that was left of her inheritance by the time the nursing home and funeral fees had been paid up. Grace felt her mother would have been pleased.

In those high school days when Grace succumbed to the dreaded dark mood swings, the jump in the river and drown days of her PMS, her mother ran her a bath and said that would make things better. Sometimes it even worked.

Soon, Grace thought, her soul too would rise up into the mist or to heaven or to God or - God forbid it should just be the final blackout. This sudden hopelessness was immeasurable. Then Grace realized that this feeling was merely a human manifestation. Her body was physical and finite. Of this Grace was certain. Beginning, middle, end.

• • •

The subway car jostled through the black underground and clattered noisily into the brightly lit station at the Museum. It came upon Grace as a surprise. In the rocking motion of the train she had been thinking about getting a decent pair of city shoes. Her hiking boots were not exactly haute couture for a job at an art gallery in Yorkville. After work she'd buy something but for now she'd have to wear her west coast walkers or hide them under the desk and go barefoot.

The train ground to a jolting halt. Grace came to. She grabbed her purse and squeezed out between the sliding doors of the subway car just as they were about to close on her. The acrid smell of the train filled her nostrils. People pushed ahead of her and for a moment she wondered if being back in the city had been the right decision. She looked ahead as the subway train rumbled off in to the dark abyss of the tunnel. There was no turning back.

• • •

Grace lay there soaking in the slowly cooling water, with a muddle of unrelated thoughts spinning in her head - frogs squashed under the tires on the way to the folk festival, old men spitting on the street while sitting on park benches outside the barber shop on Kensington Avenue, the eclipse of the moon, the feel of David's hand between her thighs, the searing cramp of her first blood red period – until the thought swam into her consciousness - by this time next week all of these mental ramblings will have disappeared like the fog burning off in the morning sun. Gone. Transformed. Intangible.

• • •

Grace walked around the corner from Bloor Street into Yorkville – it was clear - the land of the hippie generation now belonged to the baby boomers. She recognized the three story Victorian house where on more than one occasion she had sipped strong black coffee, and smoked sweet scented marijuana when it had been an all night folk haven. The problems of the world had been easily solved by the mere act of ranting and raving at the injustices of the Vietnam War and the defense of *the Freedom riders in the southern Untied States. And in the meantime the FLQ were busy trying to separate Quebec from the rest of Canada. Grace smiled at the memory of we shall overcome.*

Something had overcome Hazelton and Cumberland Streets. The hippies had moved out west or to Prince Edward Island. Some went to live on communes and others bought into the commercial three piece suit lifestyle of Bay Street. It was a phase. In a mere decade the Age of Aquarius had turned into the Age of Acquisitions. Grace was amazed at how white washed everything seemed and how the scent of cologne lingered in the air when the men brushed past her. She knew she needed more than a new pair of shoes.

20

GRACE LOOKED AT the row of shoes neatly lined up at the foot of her dresser…these boots are made for walking and that's just what they'll do….old songs faded in and out of Grace's subconscious like the times when she was four years old and she played with the dial on her parents' tube radio. The speakers hummed at different pitches with strange languages barely breaking through the short-wave frequencies.

Maybe my brain is a radio, thought Grace, and my tubes are blowing up.

• • •

That summer Faye got a portable transistor radio for her birthday. It was the same summer that all the girls wore "skorts". They looked like little pleated dresses with matching underpants sewn right in. And every sunny day that summer they lathered themselves with baby oil so they could look like Sandra Dee and then they'd pose in front of the Woolworth's Department Store in hopes of meeting a special Frankie Avalon look alike with the greased back hair. Grace thought it was disgusting. She was eight and since her hormones hadn't kicked into high gear the only good thing about that summer was listening to who put the bomp on the bomp de bomp de bomp coming out of that little transistor radio when they all went down to the beach.

• • •

How long had it been? Grace emerged out of her memories and realized that she had no clue how long she'd been sitting on the edge of the bed wondering which pair of shoes to wear. It was too cold for sandals. Her hiking boots were in the basement. They would be best for going over the trails at the park but not so great for driving. That's it - she'd wear her loafers for the drive and change into the hiking boots once she got to the Provincial Park back of Maniwaki.

Faye would expect her to take enough clothes for five days even though Grace knew she'd only needed a few things. Oh well, she whispered, five sets of underwear, five pairs of socks, two pairs of pants – one dressy and one casual, a turtle neck, two shirts, a light jacket, her flannel night gown, and sheep skin slippers. Toiletry really didn't seem necessary. Methodically Grace placed her deodorant, shampoo, nail clipper, some band aids, lip balm, and mouth wash into the transparent vanity case as if she were packing for a transatlantic flight.

This is a one way only trip of a life time, thought Grace. She closed her suitcase.

• • •

The door to the gallery swung shut behind Grace. Jason swaggered over to her and planted a kiss on her right cheek. Swinging around, he put his hands on the hips of his black leather pants and called out toward the back of the gallery, "Bryan darling, our little angel has arrived. Go get a cappuccino. You want a cappuccino, don't you? Oh, yes you do!"

Somehow when they had met out west Grace hadn't picked up on Jason's affectedness. But it didn't bother her. It was safe. And she needed that more than anything.

Jason stared at her boots. Grace shrugged, bent over to undo the laces, and pulled them off along with her grey wool socks.

"Guess these are a bit out of place here." Grace held them behind her back.

"You are a clever girl, aren't you? Well never mind. Tuck them in here." Jason opened a closet door where everything inside was fastidiously arranged. "There's a little shoe store on Bloor. We can run out at noon. I'm sure you'll find something," he said looking over his spectacles.

• • •

Grace lay her glasses down on the Quebec road map and rubbed her eyes so hard that a spectrum of light danced in psychedelic patterns on the back of her eyelids. It reminded her of OP Art or Andy Warhol or something about the Beatles. She was whipped and the morphine wasn't helping her ability to pay attention to detail.

Lately when people asked how she was doing Grace always said fine even though she felt like road kill. They really weren't interested in how she truly felt. And most times they didn't even wait for an answer. Especially at the supermarket -

How are you?

I am...fill in the blank you idiot.

That's nice. Next.

No actually, I'm dying.

Okay see you next time.

Right.

• • •

Grace flopped onto the worn sofa that faced east toward the windows of the loft apartment. Her feet were riddled with blisters from the new shoes Jason had bought for her on her lunch hour. Her shoes would break in eventually and so would her feet.

It had been a decent first day. Her job was to meet and greet the public, answer the phone, and do some shipping and receiving. Not too strenuous and not too intimidating. This could work out just fine.

Grace picked up the phone and called home.

Hi Mom......fine...yeah...I'm fine.....

• • •

Grace stared at her bare feet. She was becoming more and more detached from her body. She examined her ingrown baby toenail, the traces of fungus she'd picked up at a spa two years back, and the small bunion that made wearing dress shoes a real pain. She had feet but she was not her feet - flesh and bone - nothing more - nothing less. Her body was a capsule for the breath to come in and go out, to come in and go out, to come in and go out. To go out.

21

GRACE HAD TO get out. Ever since she rang the bell beside the grey metal door of this warehouse she now called home, it seemed that the city was slowly suffocating her feelings of belonging to the planet. It was the smell of salt from the ocean and spruce from the trees that she missed most.

   A prism of morning light streamed into the loft from the floor to ceiling windows and for a moment Grace imagined riding on one of the dust particles out to the wind where she could be swept away from the noise of the street and the smell of trash piled up on the curb. But no, gravity had her securely pinned to reality like a butterfly in a collector's scrap book.

   The sound of distant church bells wafted into her consciousness. Sunday, the day when her father lined up all of the shoes in the hall and made darned sure they were polished before sending everyone out the door to Sunday school; everyone except her father who stayed behind for a few hours of alone time or who knew what kind of time.

   Grace had to get out. Out of the loft and out of her own self. She grabbed her sketch pad and pens, and threw them into her back pack. The helmet that was strung over the handlebars of her five speed bicycle slapped against the wall as she lifted the bike over her shoulders *and headed down the stairwell into the glaring light of a hot August morning.*

• • •

Grace unbuttoned her blouse and wiped the sweat from her upper lip. She stood up from the kitchen chair and threw the window open. A gush of wind blew the map, the bus ticket, the spa brochure and other bits of paper onto the linoleum floor. Grace just stood there looking at the mess. This personal rainforest feeling that ran down her spine on a cool crisp autumn day where most folks were wearing hats and scarves could be chalked up to the cancer treatments or her age or both - menopause and chemo - a cocktail from hell.

She had been warned that this could happen. Part of the process the doctor had told her. The doctor who was all of thirty years old was a decent enough younger man with no practical experience of the hormonal shifts of women beyond the scope of medical journals and perhaps a mother who put on a purple hat and joined up with the raging grannies. But he had given Grace the morphine and when she lied and said she had lost the prescription he gave it to her again. Thanks to him she had enough for her plans.

• • •

Freedom was a gust of wind blowing her hair back from her face. Grace pedaled faster down the hill past the zoo and around the corner to Grenadier Pond at the south end of the park. It was still pretty early and only a few people were there. Grace stood straddling the cross bar of the bicycle, her heart beating in her chest, her breath slowly recovering from the exhilaration of the ride. The smell of a traffic free morning filled her lungs and for a moment she closed her eyes and imagined the sound of the swelling surf and the smell of seaweed and barnacles wrapped about the legs of the wharf.

A squirrel chattered at her as if to say you are in my territory now and the jarring sound of a distant train clattering along the lakeshore brought her mind back to her body, back to Toronto. She ached for those days with David when they went riding on his Harley along the coastal roads; when the live for the day was all they ever knew until that one day when the David disappeared - forever.

• • •

On her way up from bending over to pick up the mess on the floor Grace grabbed onto the table with both hands. The room spun in circles about her. Not again she thought. I hate Ferris wheels. I hate roller coasters. I hate this.

It had started about three years ago and the young doctor said it was loose crystals in the ear. He had taught her how to hang over the bed and shake her head until the spinning stopped. It did for while and then it came back along with blurred vision, splitting headaches and seizures. Then he got serious and ordered every test in the text book. Shortly after that Faye started taking valium to deal with the anxiety of her sister's impending doom and gloom.

It wasn't her sister's fault, thought Grace. Their mother had just been put into the nursing home, son number one had been suspended for getting the grade threes to sniff glue, and Kent had been laid off from his job at the milk plant. Things happen in threes. Her cancer made it four and that was just one too many crisis for Faye to handle.

• • •

Time lost all meaning. Sketching did that for Grace. Time stood still and slipped away all at the same time. She was completely suspended from her awareness of being and yet attuned to the world around her. It was a crazy contradiction that made complete sense. It was another one of what she called her unthinking knowing.

What was time anyway, Grace pondered as she sketched the branches of gnarly oak tree hanging over the pond. It's a measurement of space, a continuum, a theory. It's a meteor flashing through the jet black sky - one second here and another second gone. It's the rings on the trunk of an ancient sequoia. It's the memory of a lingering kiss.

"Mind if I sit here?"

A tall thirty-something year old man in madras shorts sat beside Grace and pulled on the leash as he called his wriggling spaniel over to him. "He loves ducks - can't keep him out of the water. He'd be in it all day if I let him. His name is Foster. You're...?"

Grace smiled. She knew this was one smooth move. Man has cute dog. Man goes for walk. Man sees woman. Man uses dog as bait.

"Well, Foster, I'm Grace. Who's this guy you're taking for a walk. Huh?"

"My name's Clive."

22

THE HARDEST PART about saying good bye to Clive was Grace's affection for Foster. She really had enjoyed those Sundays when Clive rang the doorbell at the loft and invited Grace to head over to the park for some squirrel and duck chasing. Grace had even bought a bag of dog goodies that she picked up at Paula's Pet Shop up on Bloor.

As for Clive - there had been one too many girls on roller blades or in jogging gear who said hello in a way that suggested he had this intimacy issue - the get close then run away approach to dating.

Still Grace was starting to feel the arousal between her thighs and whenever he called, she secretly imagined what it would be like to explore his freckled body if he asked her to. He'd already kissed her and purposely brushed against her body when they walked. He was doing the dance, the kind Grace recalled from those high school years.

Then it happened. Clive showed up around noon one Sunday. Without Foster.

• • •

The door bell rang. Grace jumped. Who would be coming over at eight o'clock at night? What if it was Faye in panic mode?

Grace fumbled to pick up the map, bus ticket and papers from under the table. She grabbed them and stuffed them into a drawer in the china cabinet.

• • •

Awkward. The whole thing was awkward - having sex with Clive. Grace couldn't get the memory of David's touch out her mind. And in that moment of Clive's ecstasy she cried, not for the joy of the pleasure as she had shared with David. She cried for her own sense of self humiliation.

Clive didn't even notice the tears. He hadn't even held her after his ejaculation. He stood up, got dressed and suggested they take the streetcar and go for Italian ice cream at College and Dovercourt. Grace said sure but in her heart she was saying what the crap have I done.

• • •

Who could it be at the door? Grace had every detail taken care of - or at least she thought she had. What had she left undone?

The bell rang again. Grace unlatch the dead bold and opened the door. It was the paper girl, Crystal. Grace was sure she had cancelled the paper last week. None of this made sense.

"Hi. I heard you were going away and I though like maybe I could like rake the leaves like while you're away maybe for a few bucks, like you know?"

Grace wondered what on earth was happening to the English language. Grace figured if computers took over the human race we'd be reduced to grunts like you know what I mean, in Neanderthal terms maybe if we're lucky, like?

"Sure, Crystal, that would be great. How's twenty bucks? The rakes are in the shed out back and the key is under the purple mums.

Say, where's Rufus?" Rufus was Crystal's Australian cow dog; it had on brown eye and one blue eye. Rufus was always with Crystal.

Grace saw that Crystal had been crying.

• • •

The Sparta Café patio was full of customers sipping strong espresso and spooning into deep scoops of Italian ice cream. It was a perfect summer day that felt more than imperfect to Grace.

"Where's Foster? How come you didn't bring him along?"

"He's with a friend? What flavor would you like? Pistachio?"

"Sure? Who?" *Grace was catching on to the tone of Clive's voice.*

"Who what?" *Clive was acting distracted. Oh boy, thought Grace. This is going to be interesting. Grace put her spoon down and tried to engage Clive.*

"Who is Foster with?"

"What does it matter?" *Clive fumbled for his money and didn't make eye contact.*

"Oh, nothing, it's just that, well..."

"Well what?" *Clive was being defensive.*

"Nothing."

"I left Foster with Angela. She's a friend from work."

• • •

Rufus had been hit by a truck. Grace couldn't think of anything to say to Crystal when she told her. No words would come.

"He's buried out behind our house, beside the willows you know over by the creek." There was a long pause from both Grace and Crystal. Finally Crystal spoke softly, "What happens when we die?"

Grace had been giving this considerable thought of late yet she didn't quite know what Crystal wanted to hear.

"I mean, do dogs have souls? Do they go to heaven?" Crystal asked innocently.

Grace gestured for Crystal to sit beside her on the front stoop. It was clear to Grace that Crystal had no idea that she had terminal cancer. Sometimes people only see what they want to see and at this moment Grace was thankful.

• • •

The small talk felt uneasy.

Grace knew that having sex with Clive had not brought them closer together. If anything she was beginning to really dislike him and hate herself for being so vulnerable.

They were about to leave when a woman wearing Ray Ban sun glasses and a tattoo of a bluebird on her shoulder leaned over the table and gave Clive a kiss. "Another conquest Clive?" Tipping the glasses down, her pinkie in the air, she smirked at Grace. "Join the club."

That was the last walk Grace had with Clive and the following Thursday when the garbage trucks came around Grace threw the dog treats out. Too bad, she thought, I liked Foster.

• • •

Grace and Crystal talked for quite a while about the meaning of life.

Grace told Crystal about her guppies that had died one summer and how they'd been flushed down the toilet. Guppies, they agreed, did not have souls. But dogs, they were different. They were faithful and especially good at keeping secrets. And some dogs were even kinder than humans. Kinder than Mr. Merkely, the janitor at the high school who called the dog catcher on the day that Rufus was on the loose doing his business on the football field. Yup. Dogs had to have souls.

Crystal thanked Grace for talking about Rufus, for agreeing that dogs have souls. Her parents were staunch Presbyterians and even though her mother had kept her brother's dead pet gerbils in the freezer all one winter until the ground was soft enough to bury them there would be no discussion about Rufus having a soul. Only humans have souls. Period. End of discussion.

Grace handed Crystal a crisp twenty dollar bill, and then said hold on a minute. She stepped inside the house for a few moments and returned with a pencil sketch she had made of Rufus about a year ago.

Crystal threw her arms around Grace's neck. She was a tall girl for 12 years of age. "I'll take good care of your lawn and when you get back we can go and visit Foster's grave."

Grace watched as Crystal slowly vanished beyond the hues of the dim street lamps and into the beginning of the rest of her journey. Crystal turned and waved good-bye.

Good-bye.

23

AT THE AGE of twelve Grace became a serious doubter. All the teachings that had been lectured to her by her permanently blonde bee-hived Sunday school teacher Mrs. MacDowell no longer seemed true. How could anybody change water into wine and then go ahead and walk on water. Even magicians were fakes. The weird guy at Faye's birthday party who was wearing a creased black tuxedo two sizes too big kept dropping the cards and when he leaned over to pull one out of Grace's head he smelled just like her father's liquor cabinet. Nothing could be trusted anymore.

On the day of Grace's confirmation she wore a frilly white dress with daisies on the translucent sleeves. Her white socks wouldn't stay even on her ankles and she'd already got a grass stain on her one-and-only-ever pair of white shoes when she ran across the field on the way to the church. Her mother had tried to wipe it off with spit and a hankie. And before the service her father kept adjusting his tie and clearing his throat. Her parents sat on a pew near the back. It was the first and last time her father had ever gone to church.

When the Anglican priest began to speak it sounded like mumbo jumbo to Grace's ears. Kneeling on her bony knees hurt but she did it obediently. She looked up at the bald man in flowing white robes. All she could do was watch his glasses jiggle on his nose. It made her giggle uncontrollably and she couldn't stop until he stared at her for what seemed to be an eternity. Surely she'd go to hell.

The last thing Grace wanted was to go to hell. At that instant she had her first epiphany. Hell? Hell did not exist. None of this existed. It was all she could do to regurgitate the catechism that she had barely memorized. From that day on the search for meaning began.

• • •

Painting soothed Grace's soul and psyche most weekends during that first year back in Toronto. From late morning to early evening the smell of oils wafted through the loft. Night time was spent consuming copious amounts of wine with the boys. They expounded on the truths and lies of life and how art was the closest thing to religion. How our existence was a complex set of uncertainties and through art the artist could internalize the complexities of being and put it forth in a new juxtaposition of images.

By September Jason arranged to have Grace's west coast paintings displayed in a bare red brick walled gallery on Queen West. It was the "nouveau district" said Bryan and he was right. More and more artists were graduating from the College of Art and were attempting to eke out a living where the rent was still cheap. Over a period of one month three of Grace's paintings sold – two to a gay couple from Germany and one to a business man from Japan. With the money Grace was able to buy enough canvases and paint to see her though the winter months.

• • •

The weather report came on at the top of the hour right after the news. Slumped on the old rocker that her mother had used when she was a baby, Grace slowly stared into the air and felt the silk red ribbon she would use to tie up the package she intended to leave for Faye. It was soothing to rub it between her thumb and forefinger, this sleek smooth ribbon. It awoke some early childhood memory that was ever so near yet, ever so just out of reach. A ribbon on the cradle perhaps?

The announcer's voice slipped in between her day dream. Snow expected over the lakehead and possibly into the Maniwaki region of Quebec on Saturday, clearing on Sunday.

Not yet. Not yet. Please don't let it snow, thought Grace. Not yet.

• • •

Working part time at the gallery in Yorkville was a contrast in demographics that Grace eventually got used to. The number of BMW's that parked illegally outside the gallery door had become common place. And people feigning more knowledge than they actually had was a test for Grace to keep her mouth shut, except to smile and say cash or credit. Tearing the customers apart was left to the midnight hours of slow burning candles in Jason and Bryan's company.

Jason warned Grace that a certain customer from Forest Hill had been to the gallery on Queen Street and she was impressed with Grace's work but she had complained that it was too west coast for her liking.

Grace choked on the cabernet and sputtered, "What!!!"

"She wants something a bit more northern Ontario if you know what I mean. Those were her words, not mine," said Jason.

"What! Scrawny shrubs that are a hundred years old?" Grace could feel her disgust rising to her temple.

"No darling," Jason drawled, "Not that far north."

"Muskoka," added Bryan, "Land of the upper-uppities." He curtsied and poured more wine.

• • •

Grace tied the silk red ribbon around the parcel neatly wrapped in white tissue paper. She stood back from the dining room table and looked at it as if to say, the last chore is done. The contents were simple — her last will and testament, a gold plated heart shaped locket with a picture of her mother on one side and her father on the other - both wearing their second world war uniforms, a list of where her paintings had been sold in the unlikely event that there would be an exhibit in a major gallery one day, and a letter for Faye.

The last thing Grace wanted was for Faye to bear the guilt of her final decision to leave this way. Lord knows Faye felt responsible for all acts requiring some sort of remorse of regretful forthcomings. She'd always been like that even when they were in public school. Like the time Grace got caught lighting matches in the girls' washroom, Faye somehow took on the burden of responsibility. This trait had been etched into her ego her whole life and had been transmitted onto her children so that they no longer took responsibility for their own shortcomings. Grace did not want Faye to take on the weight of this decision. It had nothing to do with Faye. But Grace still had her doubts that the letter would work.

24

THE GREY HAZE of the September morning lay heavy upon the cityscape. Grace was in a frantic mood. In her hurry to get out the door and head downtown to the gallery on Queen Street, Grace nearly stepped on the letter that lay on the tiled floor of the vestibule. She'd almost missed it. More important things were on her mind, like the fact that her exhibit had run its course and it was time to dismantle everything and bring back the paintings that didn't sell.

With a recalcitrant sigh Grace plunked down on the stairs not unlike a sack of potatoes. She ripped open the envelope and a check fell into her lap. It was from the Dame of Muskoka as Jason had dubbed her. The advance on her first commission had arrived. The sheer exhilaration of joy jumped into Grace's body causing her to do an impromptu dance resembling a hybrid between that of the Funky Chicken and a pirouette. Grace tucked the check into her wallet; as she dashed out the door to catch the street car, she felt giddy all over. She began to calculate umpteen ways she could spend the advance – a massage, a new bicycle, a popcorn maker, a trip home to see her mother - and then the reality hit home like a baseball being fired at her gut.

My God I've got to paint something that resembles Muskoka.

. . .

Every room was in order. It had never been this neat, not even when the whole family had come over for cooked ham last Easter. But it felt right. Grace had taken time to make it right. Not by choice but by condition. The simplest chores that she had been able to do a year ago now sapped her of all her strength. It was as if her energy had gone on vacation but like an old piece of luggage her body had been left behind. So what once would have taken a few hours, took days to do. Even catching the dust bunnies under her bed was enough work for one day.

The cancer seemed alien by times; not a part of her own doing but some sort of foreign invasion. It reminded Grace of the summer when a leech had latched onto her left foot right between her toes. She'd picked it up when the neighborhood kids had gone swimming in the river on her eighth birthday. It sucked the blood right out of her and Grace was sure she was going to die. But she lived - despite the pain that made her cry when her father took it off.

She was going to die. The medical judgment had been confirmed in the sterility of the doctor's office. The words were less than sympathetic - it's a matter of time now; make your plans.

After the initial shock, after going through all the stages of denial, anger and self loathing Grace came up with the plan. She would not put anyone through the agony of watching her wither up like that stupid leech. She'd make sure of that.

• • •

The Group of Seven paintings haunted Grace for weeks as she tried to come to terms with the right concept for the Dame of Muskoka, who was in fact a retired drama teacher. Her real name was Edith Wilcox and her husband had made his fortune in the newspaper business.

Finally, after a late night of bacchanalian drinking and dancing at the El Mocombo on Spadina, Grace slipped into a surrealistic world of dreaming and waking, dreaming and waking. In the morning she put on Miles Davis' Sketches of Spain and made a pot of Columbian coffee. She painted for five hours straight. Splashes of aqua intertwined with green, vermillion, yellow, white and gold. It was a swirling orchestration of color; a rhythmic response in light and dark. It was her first abstract. It won the heart of Edith Wilcox whose husband's pocket book was freely flowing.

• • •

Every cent had been accounted for. Even the loony jar that Grace had stashed behind the cook books in case of an emergency lay empty on the kitchen counter. Several weeks ago she'd wrapped them up into three rolls. Two went to the local food bank and the other one she gave to the paper girl.
 "Wow. How come?" Crystal was delighted.
 "Because," said Grace, "you deserve it."

• • •

Self worth was an attribute that Grace did not come by easily. There were times when she knew it and still couldn't figure out how to get over it and get on with life, until she went out west with David and seriously embraced painting. It was a turning point. Life took on meaning. Everything in the universe had a purpose and an order. Hers was to paint.
 Lately, like a planet spinning in retrograde motion, Grace fell into self loathing and deception. It pulled her core down deeper than the agony she had felt on the day of her confirmation. Resurfacing seemed impossible. But not unlike the cruel shifting of hormones, she survived. Then when Mrs. Wilcox told Grace how enthralled she was with her talents, Grace's confidence took flight once again and she was inspired to paint more.
 The commissions kept Grace afloat to the point that she was able to move on from the Muskoka paintings to her Tree of Life series. In one

year she picked up two juried awards and was given a sizeable grant from the Toronto Arts Council to create a mural for a new housing and arts coop being built on recovered factory lands down by Cherry Beach. It was at the height of this success that she stood on the precipice of yet another great tumble.

Faye called in hysterics. Their mother had been in a car accident out on the second concession. A cement mixer hogging the road had forced her to swerve into the ditch. The night of David's accident flashed in Grace's mind as Faye spoke without taking a breath.

"The car's a write off Grace. You've got to come home. Mom is in the hospital with a broken pelvis. My God Grace you know what they say when old people break a hip. They die within a year. Not that Mom's going to die or anything. Grace you've got to come home. I mean move home. This is just too much to handle now with the three kids raising hell and Kent's never around and well you know I'm doing my best but Jesus Grace say something.

25

SILENCE HUMMED IN Grace's head resembling a telephone left off the hook or the late night white noise of the 1958 TV set that dominated her parent's living room on Chestnut Street. The call of a blue jay outside the window broke her last moment of just being in her modest townhouse on the west end of town.

It still amazed her that she had been able to buy her own house on the income from selling her art, that along with the summer courses she taught at the community college. Pain pay, she called it. Teaching did not come naturally to Grace but she forgave herself for this short coming and guiltlessly used the institutional payments to reduce the mortgage.

Grace had no idea how long she had been standing motionless in the middle of her eclectic living room. Slowly she turned around three hundred and sixty degrees. It was a technique she had unconsciously adapted when going to art galleries. She long ago stopped following the crowds viewing in order one picture at a time for a few mere seconds. Instead she would go to the centre of the room, turn slowly and be drawn into the overall sensation of the artistic expressions. Only when a certain picture spoke to her heart would she be drawn toward the perimeter. *Stop twirling Grace, you'll hurt your head.*

A detachment crept over her and the room grew dark as a passing cloud masked the autumn sunlight. She stopped assessing the gallery of her material life as she once knew it, turned on the stereo, and slowly sagged down onto the soft burgundy sofa. Without blinking, without thinking, Grace stared outside the picture window at the leaves falling in syncopation to the Mozart bassoon concerto being performed live from London. Peace will come.

• • •

Leaving Toronto wasn't the problem. Neither was the deep desire Grace had had to help her mother. The boys held a farewell bash in the loft and most of the arts crowd showed up, partly to say goodbye to Grace, partly to schmooze with Jason and Brian in hopes of getting an exhibit at their gallery, and mostly for the free flowing alcohol.

The real problem for Grace was would she be able to fit in where she hadn't been since she turned eighteen? Anyone she'd known in high school had left for university or they followed their dreams to some faraway place like Tibet or Peru. Everyone she'd hung around with had been chomping on the bit to get out this two bit town with its one bowling alley, its derelict drive in theatre and dead end future. Those who stayed behind ended up married with kids and a mortgage that left them tied to the assembly line at one of the three dying factories still left in town after the free trade agreement messed everything up.

No, leaving Toronto wasn't the problem. Grace had never fully embraced it as what one might call home. It came out of an artistic necessity, first as a student and later when David died, and at the time there seemed to be no other place to go.

• • •

Grace was ready to go. The car was packed and there was nothing left to do except to go. The phone rang.

Shit. Grace knew it would be Faye making a last minute check.

"So are you sure you don't want me to drive you to the bus station."

"No, Faye. I mean, yes, I'm sure, I'm okay. Oh, look, the taxi is pulling up." Grace swallowed her lie. "Got to go. Don't worry. Yes, I'll call you tonight when I get checked in. Promise."

"Promise?"

"Promise."

"Swear?"

"Swear. Geesh Faye we're in our fifties not our teens. Look the taxi guy is waving at me. I'll miss my bus." Another lie.

"Okay then, call me tonight."

"I will. I will." Silence stepped in between them. "Faye?"

"Yeah?"

"Love you."

"Love you too."

IV

A seed hidden in the heart of an apple is an orchard invisible.

~Welsh Proverb

26

THE CRIMSON-COLORED MORNING shone through the classroom window on that September day when Mrs. Appleton announced to her grade three class that they would be collecting leaves for their science project. "Trees," said Grace's teacher as she smoothed back her graying hair, "Are the life blood of our planet. They give us oxygen so that we can breathe. Without trees there would be no life on earth."

. . .

So far, it had been a warm autumn and there were many multi-colored leaves barely touched by the frost that still swayed on the maples along the driveway at Grace' house. The trip will be beautiful, thought Grace.

Taking a slow, deep breath Grace put the keys into the ignition and the engine turned over. Three months had passed since Grace had last driven and for a split second she felt a damp rush of uncertainty in the palm of her hands. Then she backed the car out of the drive and headed up the street toward the north end of town.

. . .

The old shoe box was filled with leaves of every hue - red, yellow, orange, brown and muted green. That weekend after Mrs. Appleton announced the truth about trees - that they give us life - Grace had gone out to the woods beyond the back fields that lay behind her parent's post war home to collect dozens of leaves - maple, birch, oak, beechnut, poplar, and sumac.

On her way back to the house she walked through the dried up brittle remains of the mowed hayfield. A distant chorus of honking geese came from the north and Grace stopped to gaze up at the "V" formation as they passed overhead. Soon all the leaves will be gone, thought Grace. Soon the trees will fall asleep.

• • •

Driving a car is as easy as getting back on a bike, mused Grace as she pulled up to a red light on the highway leading out of town. This won't be that bad.

She looked in the rear view mirror. A police cruiser had come to a halt a few feet behind her bumper. Oh shit. Act normal. Smile. Be cool. Damn it. Grace clutched the steering wheel with her sweating palms.

The light turned green. Cautiously Grace stepped on the gas pedal and proceeded through the intersection. She glanced in the mirror. Still there. She flicked on the turn signal and took the next right. Again she checked the mirror. The cruiser hadn't followed her. A few yards up the street Grace stopped the car, dropped her shoulders, and gave out a sigh of relief. Onward and upward, she said out loud, onward and up.

• • •

While her mother set up the ironing board Grace spread the leaves out on the old pine kitchen table. At the time Grace had no idea that this would be a special moment that she would revisit over and over again throughout her life; the day she and her mother were at peace with the world, and with one another.

"Get out the wax paper and we'll coat the leaves to preserve them." Her mother plugged the old iron into the socket beside the fridge. "And get out that tattered tea towel at the back of the drawer. That'll do fine," she said. "We don't want to ruin the new ones we got from your Aunt Gloria last Christmas."

It was a perfect Sunday afternoon. Faye had gone over to her girlfriend's to watch soaps and Grace's father had gone off for some last of the fishing season with the boys. It was just the two of them. Grace and Lillian, her Mom.

The smell of roast beef cooking in the oven and apples stewing on the stove filled the kitchen. Together they slowly pressed each leaf between two sheets of wax paper. It was the kind of day when the truth was told about the life her mother had lived when she was a girl; stories about the great depression and how when her Mom was little, she and her three brothers and two sisters had to struggle to get enough food for the week; stories about catching bullheads in the back ponds; stories about the men who hopped on freight trains and came begging at the back door; stories about picking wild berries in the farmers' field and never getting caught.

• • •

Grace had no intention of getting caught. She'd brought along her expired driver's license just in case. If she got pulled over, her story would be that she had forgotten to renew it. She'd been out of the country. And oh, my goodness, how foolish of me, officer, I really must take care of this right away. It was a lie so she had rehearsed it several times, asking herself questions like, where had she been. Spain would be the answer. She'd done an art tour of Madrid, Granada and Barcelona back in the eighties so at least this would be half true.

Last week Grace had meticulously marked her route out on the maps of Ontario and Quebec in bright yellow highlighter. Wherever possible Grace planned to stick to the secondary roads, besides the countryside would be glorious at this time of year and there really was no urgency to get anywhere. After all no one was expecting her. And as far as she knew, no one suspected her true intention.

• • •

They used an old photo album for Grace's collection of leaves. All that afternoon while the apples simmered on the stove and they patiently waxed each leaf, Grace listened to her mother's olden day stories.

At one point Grace took a bright red maple to the window and pressed it so that the autumn light shone through. All the veins stood out. It reminded Grace of the time she had put her hands over the glaring light of the flashlight they kept in the hall closet. She could see all of her finger bones and blood vessels glowing in a bright red silhouette.

27

THE CRUMBLING BUILDINGS on the outskirts of town gave way to the open expanse of farmers' fields. Grace wanted to look around at everything the way she had done when the family had packed a picnic and headed north to their favorite sandy beach. Keeping her attention on the oncoming traffic was harder than she had anticipated. The car felt as if it was floating on air and Grace knew it wasn't but her lightheadedness made it seem that way. When she realized that she had been gripping the steering wheel for dear life she laughed out loud and let go with both hands for a fraction of a second, daring the car to drive on its own.

At that moment a motorcycle revved its engine and flashed by on the driver's side. Grace seize the wheel. The car veered toward the shoulder but Grace regained control once more. After the initial shock Grace reached down with her right hand and turned on an oldies station on the car radio. "Take a piece of my heart now darling; Take a piece of my heart..."

• • •

"There's a tree in the root in the hole in the bottom of the sea". The whole family was singing their way to the beach. Even Grace's

parents were singing and counting the cows in the fields as their old rusting blue Dodge made its way along the twisting country roads. They'd stuffed rags in the gaps in the floor boards but the dust still filtered in.

Every Saturday in the summer when the weather permitted Grace and Faye helped their mother make the picnic lunch while her father gathered up the lawn chairs, the charcoal and the beach blankets. Then he'd top up the leaking radiator with water from an old milk bottle in hopes that they'd all make it to the beach. There were egg salad sandwiches, bologna slices, carrots and celery, dill pickles, lemonade, apples, peanut butter and jelly sandwiches and sometimes oatmeal cookies made on Friday night.

Faye usually brought her battery operated transistor radio with its single ear plug. Grace's parents insisted she not use it in the car so that they could all sing together. Faye would sulk for a little while until Grace got her going with a game of "I spy". Scamper, the wiry fox terrier that could never sit still, panted and wriggled the whole time between Faye and Grace. Sometimes it would race back and forth from one window to the other and occasionally try to jump into the front seat.

"Lillian, keep that blasted dog back there," barked Grace's father. It was an innocent time and it was mostly happy.

• • •

The rambling rural roads outside of town were still familiar to Grace. In some ways nothing had changed since the sixties; the same old barns stood in disrepair, the foundations of abandoned cheese factories were barely visible beneath the overgrowth of shrubs and weeds, and the old railway line crisscrossed the county road every few miles - a reminder of a time when fewer people owned cars. A few modern bungalows had cropped up here and there on the lands that the farm families sold when their children moved away and there was no one to take over. Seemed like the only farmers to make a go of it were the ones who had bought into the agricultural industry of biogenetics. The age of subsistent survival was rapidly fading away.

Grace wondered about the perfectly square tomatoes she had seen in the fresh produce aisle of the supermarket. Maybe they were easier to pack, but were they good for you. Whatever happened to those tomatoes that were purple? And just maybe a scab on an apple was better than a pesticide covered waxy red delicious shipped in from some distant and chemically controlled apple orchard.

• • •

It wasn't her fault that her parents panicked when they couldn't find her. She'd wandered off from the beach to use the outhouse. That's when Grace saw the unkempt apple orchard across the road. She went exploring, that's all. She could still see her family at the far end of the park, her father practicing horseshoes, her mother knitting and Faye lying on her beach towel, the one with Surfs Up written in bright red letters and a cartoon of a girl in a blue bikini. One day, Grace thought, when I'm thirteen, I'll have boobs, and I'll have a bikini too.

Grace walked up to a gnarly apple tree. There were late summer apples hanging from the branches. She knew she should go back but there was a voice. Was it the tree or was it her imagination? She couldn't tell. It said, climb me. My apples are free. They're for you. Climb me.

• • •

A sudden urge for homemade apple pie grumbled in Grace's stomach. Maybe, she thought, if she took a little side step to the village with the stone bridge, maybe the country diner would still be open. It was after Thanksgiving and most things closed up for the season once the fishing was done and the tourists from Pennsylvania and New York State had gone home for another year.

Grace drove the car around the curve and downhill toward the village. She passed the old red brick schoolhouse that now served as someone's home. The new windows and geranium filled garden made it look lovely, thought Grace. It would make a great painting studio. For brief moment Grace allowed herself to dream of a possibility that would no longer become a reality.

• • •

The boughs of the apple tree cradled Grace and the breeze lulled her mind to a place where fairytales came alive. She was a princess in a castle garret waiting for her prince to slay the dragon. She had no idea that her parents were frantically looking for her. It never occurred to Grace that they thought that she had wandered off and had become lost or worse yet, had somehow, when they weren't looking, waded into the water and drowned.

The apple with worm holes and scabs was deliciously tart and the juice tricked onto her chin as she bit into it. Grace would surprise her mother. She'd bring back as many as she could carry in the lap of her folded over blouse. They could stew them up for Sunday supper.

But the surprise was not for Grace's parents it was for Grace. It was the scolding she got from her mother and the sting of her father's belt on her backside. She was never to do that again. Never. That day Grace learned that some things like fairytale apple orchards are better kept as a secret.

28

SEEING THE VILLAGE again brought a flood of memories to Grace's mind; memories of summer secrets. Secrets she never told her parents.

Suddenly Grace remembered being thirteen when she met this older girl from Montreal who was staying in the trailer park where Grace and her family were having their picnic. They stole a pack of cigarettes from the canteen and smoked them out behind the change rooms. When Grace threw up she blamed it on the hot dogs.

And then there was the week after going all the way with Terry. There was no way in heaven or hell that Grace was going to tell her parents she might be pregnant, like what had happened to Faye. Grace had long ago learned that not telling was the best option.

Grace pulled the car up alongside the paint-chipped, faded red bench perched in front of the Waterfalls Diner. She got out, locked the car door behind her, and she slowly glanced around as if the village were some sort of abstract representation of a place where people actually lived. And, no, it wasn't a movie set - though it could be thought Grace - good for a murder mini-series.

It looked mostly the same as when she was a kid - its row of lonely houses losing all hope of being cared for, the gas station store without gas pumps still being used to sell live bait for those fishing for pike or bass, and the whitewashed Orange Lodge as a gruesome reminder of the Irish Protestants who long ago settled on the miserable lands not already claimed by earlier settlers.

    The screen door with the Ginger Ale crossbar slammed behind Grace announcing her entrance into the diner. The whole place reeked of greasy fries and onions. Grace sat on a 1960's chrome chair with a yellow plastic backrest and cracked cushion that had been sat on one too many times. A frayed piece of grey electrical tape ran over a protruding rip on the seat. The wobbly table was covered with a sticky plastic tablecloth. Grace pushed the over-used ketchup bottle and smudged salt and pepper shakers to one side. There was a hand printed card with the daily specials written on it including a misspelled "punkin" pie. It felt familiar but different. There were no other customers. Then Grace remembered how late it was in the season.

    "What'll it be ma'am?"

    Grace tried not to stare at the girl's protruding stomach that caused her soiled white waitress uniform to ride up in the front. By Grace's estimation she couldn't be more than sixteen and she was about seven months pregnant.

    "What'll it be ma'am?"

• • •

"It should be my baby." Bryan downed the last of his cabernet in one huge swallow.

    "It'll have your nose, my God, Bryan, you wouldn't want that." Jason crossed his legs and swung his foot back in forth in a taunting motion. *"It should be mine. Grace, you decide. You're the one who'll carry the child."*

    "Boys, boys, boys. I love you both, you know I do". Grace had lost count of the number of glasses of wine she'd consumed since Jason cooked supper, a ritual for most Saturday nights after a long week at the gallery.

"And you're both so handsome but having a fetus growing inside is well, weird. I know it's supposed to be natural and all but really, I don't know."

It wasn't the first time the boys said they wanted to be fathers. "Artificial insemination was working for lots of straight people," they said, "why not for a loving, gay couple like us? And we are so fond of you. You're artistic and intelligent. You'd be a perfect match."

At this point Grace hugged them both, said, "Goodnight darlings, and I promise to come back in the morning to help with the dishes."

Grace went across the hall to the emptiness of her own loft apartment where, by the shadows of the street lights cascading across her bed, she cried herself to sleep.

• • •

"It's a boy." The waitress caressed the orb of her own stomach.

Grace fumbled for a word.

"I saw you look. It's no secret. My great granny's excited 'cause she's going to be a great-great grandma. Yup, and me and Lloyd, we're getting ourselves a mobile home back of the lake there. Just think, a baby for Christmas. You got any kids?"

"No, no children." Grace tried not to stare.

"Oh really, that's a shame. I didn't plan this but you know how it goes." The waitress giggled and cracked her gum at the same time. Then she leaned into Grace as if she were telling a secret. "Like he didn't use anything if you know what I mean." She straightened up, her hand on her back. "Well, anyway what'll it be? We got punkin pie on special."

"Do you have apple pie?"

"Do we have apple pie?" The girl bent over to wipe of the plastic table cloth with her ammonia tainted dish rag, Grace could see the cleavage of the girl's swelling breasts. "Do we have apple pie? Do dogs shit on the beach?"

Grace felt sorry for the girl. Even though she seemed happy, it made Grace feel sad; sad because how could any young woman not want to explore her own life before having an accidental child. Sad because there was a part of Grace that wished she had had her own child to love and be loved by. Then she remembered Faye's kids and the thought flew right out of her mind.

• • •

That night after the great baby debate with the boys Grace's bed sloshed from side to side and the alcohol oozed out of her pores. In her dreams she was riding an elevator. She was completely naked from the waist down but none of the people on the elevator could see her. Then she was rowing a boat in an underground tunnel. A voice kept saying go to the light, go to the light. By this time the mid morning sun was streaming onto her pillow and Grace had no choice but to get up and stand in a cold shower.

The water ran over her body and Grace rehashed the previous evening's discussion of her being a surrogate mother. She loved Jason and Bryan in a sisterly, brotherly sort of way. But it wasn't the same kind of love that she and David had discovered between and within each other, the kind of love that comes once in a lifetime. It was the one and only time that she had wanted to have a child, to share their lives with, to teach and to learn from.

No, Grace could not be the one to bear a child for her dearest of dear friends. She would tell them later that afternoon.

29

IT WAS ALREADY noon. Grace knew she needed to get to the motel by supper, to call Faye on time, to keep the plan on track. She glanced again at the diner's teapot shaped wall clock with a cartoon-like face that reminded her of Captain Kangaroo. There was time.

Grace looked around. The diner had everything a camper or the weekend cottage-goers would want but not necessarily need. Next to the canned beans and spaghetti in tomato sauce were marshmallows and chips. There was a first aid shelf with sunscreen for the UV rays, bug repellent to ward off the horseflies, black flies and deer flies, ointment for cuts and bruises, and aspirin for the hangovers. To the left of the snack bar stood a magazine rack that was mostly empty except for a few comic books, a fishing guide and an already well read woman's magazine with something on the cover about the royal family and a UFO sighting. The window display boasted faded packages of rubber worms for wannabe fishermen, several packages of fireworks, a butterfly net, and three kinds of beaded moccasins.

Grace walked up to the cash register on the counter and looked at the crooked plastic Cola sign over the grill. It boasted four flavors of ice-cream – chocolate, vanilla, maple walnut and strawberry ripple. At either end of the snack bar two dessert cases displayed the local sweets, one with cupcakes in dripping pink icing sugar, the other with a half eaten apple pie. A bluebottle the size of a dime sat on the cover.

The waitress leaned sideways on the cash register with one hand on the back of her hips and the other on the round of her stomach. Grace handed her a five dollar bill and indicated with a smile that she didn't need any change.

"He's going to be a dancer or a foot ball player. Least that's what I think, cause boy he can kick. My doctor had to move him around twice already. Don't want him coming out feet first he said."

• • •

They said they understood. Jason and Bryan sat on their art deco divan, Bryan's arm around Jason's shoulder.

"I, I, can't have a baby right now." Sometimes Grace stuttered when she was nervous. It's just that, that, that I have this mural I'm doing for the coop. Grace felt horrible that she was disappointing her two best friends in the world. "And well…"

"No need to explain." Jason smiled. "Besides, we've been looking into adopting."

Within three weeks Bryan and Jason set up an appointment with an adoption agency and within four weeks Bryan got the results from the lab. He was HIV positive.

• • •

It was in the bottom drawer of her parents' dresser. The picture. Grace's mother had left her in the bedroom when she had crossed the hall to make the beds that Faye and Grace had slept in the night before. Faye was at school and Grace being the curious four year old that she was had managed to open the drawer and discovered a number of things she had never seen before including a tube with a bulb on it that she later learned as an adult was a douche.

The yellow cotton and embroidered hankie caught her eye. She pulled it out and unfolded each corner carefully as if she were opening the wings of a dead bird. It was a picture of a tiny baby boy wrapped in a blue blanket. His eyes were closed as if he was dreaming in the land of Winken, Blinken and Nod, thought Grace.

"Mommy, mommy, look a baby."

• • •

Two local boys, one in a blue baseball cap that read "Farmers do it in the Field", the other with bright red hair and a face full of left over summer freckles brushed by Grace as she swung open the diner's screen door.

Walking toward her car, Grace over heard one of the boys call out, "Hey sugar babe."

And the waitress replied, "Lloyd you looser, get over here."

Grace wondered which of the boys was Lloyd, which one was the looser, which one really fathered the baby? Would it be born with red hair or a baseball cap?

• • •

Tears welled in her mother's eyes. Grace had never seen her mother cry before and it made her think that she had done something really bad. Really, really bad, but what? She held the picture up to her mother.

"It's baby Sam." Grace's mother took the picture in one hand and pulled a handkerchief out of the pocket of her apron with her other hand and wiped her tears.

"Who's Sam?"

Grace's mother knelt down and sat on the floor beside Grace. She took hold of the photograph and cradled the picture in the palm of her hands. "He's your baby brother."

I've got a baby brother, thought Grace and a surge of excitement raced though her body. "Where's Sam now? Where is he?"

"Sam's in heaven, Gracie"

"In heaven? Where's heaven Mommy? Can we go and see him?"

Silence lingered over Grace for what seemed to be a forever and ever moment. Then her mother explained how her brother had only lived for a few short days before his heart stopped beating. Grace wondered why a baby would ask his heart to stop beating but she didn't ask her mother why. Her mother told her more, and the more she told Grace, the more Grace wanted to know.

Sam was buried beneath a willow tree at the cemetery. Cemeteries were where dead people went? Yes, but no, said Lillian. There were so many questions that morning. Was heaven in the cemetery? Why do babies die? Do we get to chose when we die? If heaven isn't in the cemetery where is heaven? Does Jesus have a home like ours in heaven?

That afternoon Grace curled up in her mother's arms like a teaspoon against a tablespoon and they fell asleep to the call of blue jays outside the bedroom window. It was the last time Grace remembered her mother holding her that way.

• • •

When Grace walked into their loft apartment that Friday evening, as she always did, with a bottle of wine ready to contribute to the frivolity of the weekend, she knew immediately that things were amiss. Bryan was sobbing in Jason's arms.

AIDS was still a new but dreaded word in the homosexual community. That night the mood went from somber to the ridiculous. At times all three of them were engulfed in silly fits of laughter and then they cried and poured more of the medicinal vintage. No matter what was going to happen, they agreed, they would get through this. They would beat the virus and it would not get in the way of living life to its fullest.

30

A LIGHT RAIN splashed against the windshield. Grace turned on the wipers and drifted away in thought to the steady syncopation of the blades.

The idea of immortality seeped slowly into her subconscious. It was a popular theme at university; that and other utopian idealisms. The search for the unattainable. The longing for Nirvana, Valhalla, or Shangri-La. The back to the land post war babies turned hippy philosophers. And now that she was certain of her own destiny she began to wonder why it was that humanity had not yet found a way to eradicate the world of hunger, disease, pestilence, and war. Why had the cancer taken over her body? The guilt of her Anglicanism, the confusion of the catechism, and the erroneous blessing of the beautiful beatitudes wafted through her unconscious state as the windows began to steam up.

The tail lights of the car in front of her suddenly flashed red. Grace jumped back to being one with her car and slammed on the brakes. The car skidded on the wet pavement and came to a full stop. In a split second Grace saw the flash of the animal's white tail. A deer. She watched the graceful animal lope across the rain soaked field.

It's time hasn't come, she thought. It's time hasn't come.

• • •

Grace and the boys watched the moving van pull away from the loft. All of Grace's few worldly possessions and her expertly packed paintings had been loaded and were on their way to her new house in the hometown back east.

"We'll be fine Gracie-girl. You've got to be there for your mother and we'll be here whenever you want to come back for a visit." Bryan was ever the optimist even though the AIDS had wasted him down to a mere shadow of his former self, and his face was covered with sores that weren't healing. Jason smiled and put his arm around Bryan but the look in his eyes told another story - one of sorrow and fear.

"Keep the futon ready! I'll be back, and Bryan, stay away from eating all those sweets. You'll get fat." Grace made a feeble attempt to make light of a dismal situation. "And Jason, thank you for everything. These past nine years have been incredible. If it hadn't been for you giving me a chance to work at the Gallery and…"

"Never mind, never mind. Now go. You'll miss your train." Jason shooed his hand at Grace. "Go. Oh shit, I hate good-byes."

The three hugged for a brief time without end. No words. Grace hoisted up her shoulder bag, grabbed her suitcase and made her way down the stairs to the front door. Looking back up the stairwell toward her dearest friends, all that Grace could see of them was a silhouette against the glare of the back light shining from their apartment.

"Go," they chorused.

"Okay, I'm going." Grace called back.

As soon as she stepped out of the building she was able to flag a blue and black taxi that happened to be passing by at that exact moment. It whisked Grace away from the loft, away from her friends and away from her life as she had known it up to that time.

• • •

The close encounter with the deer embedded itself like a dull knife in the back of Grace's nervous system. Not only was she rattled but the car's gas gauge was getting too close to empty. And the uncertainty of finding a gas station sooner than later played tricks on her sense of self-assuredness.

There's got to be one in the next village, she thought drumming her fingers on the steering wheel. Her stomach was turning into knots and her head began to throb. No, no, no, no, no. With her right hand Grace fumbled through her purse for the bottle of morphine capsules. Taking it in her right hand she began to unscrewed the lid with her teeth. The car hit a pot hole and the pills flew out in every direction. No, no, no, no, no.

A lightning bolt of pain flashed behind her eyes. Grace pulled over to the side of the road. The tires skidded and the wet gravel shot up into the air. The car came to a stop and in a convulsion Grace flopped over the steering wheel, the engine still running.

• • •

The rocking motion of the train and the fleeting images of Lake Ontario lulled Grace into a somnambulant dreamland. All of her memories became blurred and distorted. Feelings of loving and longing intermingled with the fear of not knowing; missing David, still after all these years, and wondering if she had told him how much she had loved him; worrying about Bryan and wishing she could change his journey; distressing about her mother and not knowing who would take care of her now that she was confined to a wheel chair; fretting about her future as an artist, and how would she survive living outside of her supportive arts community.

"Coffee, tea, juice?"

The steward rolled the tray up the aisle and stopped beside Grace's seat. He repeated in his Quebecois accent, "Coffee, tea, juice?"

"Nothing right now. Thank you. Merci."

• • •

Spit drooled from her mouth. Grace slowly came to and straightened up in the seat. The car's lights were on but the engine wasn't running. The gas tank indicator was on empty. Her pills were scattered all over the seat beside her and on the floor under the gas pedal. She could hear a muffled ringing of the cell phone Faye had insisted she take with her.

That would be Faye checking in on her. What would she say? Nothing. Absolutely nothing. Grace ignored the ringing. She had to get to a gas station and get back on the road.

Grace looked ahead. A rusty brown pickup truck was backing up on the side of the road toward her car. Grace's instinct was to lock all her doors but then she realized she didn't have much choice but to hope that whoever this was, was going to help her get some gas.

"You okay ma'am?" A pimply faced young man in farmer's overalls knocked on the car window.

Grace shouted from behind her car window, "I've run out of gas."

"You're in luck, there's a station just a couple miles down the road. I can take you there."

31

THE INSIDE OF the pickup truck smelled distinctly like manure, probably stuck on the boots from a day in the barn, thought Grace. The acne scarred young man said his name was Bobby, like Bobby Orr on account that his father had played defense for the Pembroke Lumber Kings and once Bobby Orr had come to town for a charity game and signed autographs for everybody.

Bobby said he was on his way to get a part for his tractor from the co-op in town so it wasn't out of his way and he'd be glad to give Grace a ride back to her car on his way back out of town. He'd only be about a half an hour give or take a few minutes, depending who was on cash because if it was Chantal well, he wanted to ask her to the dance at the Legion this Saturday night.

Grace was thankful that Bobby had a gift of the gab even though at times she had trouble understanding his valley accent. It was tinged with a distortion of Irish going back to the long ago days when they had fled the ravages of the potato famine and settled on the rocky wastelands around Lanark County. At least she didn't have to explain anything about herself and that was good.

Grace looked at the layer of dust on the dash that seemed to float up into the air with every bump in the road. The shocks were gone, laughed Bobby, but one day he was going to get himself a brand new

GMC with the works, just as soon as he sold off the back acres to some filthy rich dude out of Ottawa. They can have the swamp for all he cared. Fill it in and good riddance to those god damn gad nippers.

Grace looked confused.

Mosquitoes.

• • •

That summer Grace's family rented a cottage on one those swampy lakes two hours north of town. And that summer Grace discovered her allergy to insect bites. She and Faye had been swimming and paddling all day. The deer flies were all over them and by the time they came in for supper Grace's joints were swollen and her eyes were practically closed. Her whole body was puffed up like the Pillsbury dough boy.

Grace's mother had a panic attack right in the middle of making macaroni and cheese, Grace's favorite. She insisted that Grace be taken to a doctor in the nearest village, some ten miles away by dirt road. And everyone was going. Everyone, even the dog.

About thirty minutes later Grace's father pulled the car up to a huge Victorian house with shutters falling off their hinges. At the side of the building there was an addition for the doctor's office. Grace's mother ordered everyone to stay put and then she grabbed Grace by her swollen arm and proceeded to the door. There was an old fashioned door bell that Grace's mother turned and turned and turned.

Finally a woman in a black dress came to the door and said that the doctor was eating his dinner and couldn't come right away. By this point Grace's mother was hysterical seeing as Grace's whole face looked like a balloon about to burst. She pushed past the woman and dragged Grace into the dining room where indeed the doctor and his family were eating their dinner.

It ended up that all Grace needed was a shot in the butt and a package of antihistamines. He recommended chamomile lotion for the itch and suggested that Grace stay indoors or if she really wanted to go outside she would have to be covered up from head to foot. Being embarrassed by her mother was worse than the bug bites. Grace never forgot that summer.

• • •

Sitting in the wheelchair facing the window Grace's mother didn't hear her daughter come into the tiny rose-colored room in the Riverview Nursing Home. Grace saw the hearing aids lying on the night stand. Not again, she thought. Lately her mother had taken to refusing to wear them saying all she could hear was a bunch of noise.

Grace picked up the hearing aids and went around where she could face her aging mother. She held them out with one hand and pointed to her own ears to indicate that her mother should put them in.

"Good," she shouted, "You try wearing them for a change." And then, "How are you Faye."

"It's Grace, Mom and I'm fine." Grace bent over and gave her mother a kiss on the cheek.

Some days were better than others. The time travel didn't bother Grace; it actually helped the conversation move along. Then one day Grace's mother looked at her daughter with great uncertainty and said, "Is your father still alive? How come he doesn't come to see me?"

Grace's heart stuck fast in her throat and she tried not to cry. She took hold of her mother's hands to offer some comfort. "Well Mom, Dad passed away some years back. Remember?"

"Well damn him anyway. He's always been up to no good."

• • •

Grace knew that Faye would be getting anxious; she'd already called twice on the cell phone and Grace needed to call her back but what would she say? Oh, I passed out at the side of the road and couldn't talk just then. And then, I ran out of gas and this complete stranger picked me up and I'm at a gas station in the middle of who-knows-wheresville. Don't worry.

The gas station looked like it had last seen the bristle end of a paintbrush twenty or thirty years ago. Right below a faded billboard for Good Year Tires on the east side of the garage was a wooden bench that had seen its fair share of bad weather. Grace sat on it.

"I'll be back in two shakes of a dead lamb's tail," said the farmer, "and I'll get you back on the road. Where'd you say you were headed?"

"North."

32

"THE BUS RIDE is fine."

Grace hated telling untruths but it was her only way out. Faye wanted to know why Grace hadn't answered the phone when she called - twice.

"I met this farmer guy." At least this was true. "And he had so much to tell me about his name being Bobby like Bobby Orr. And you know, Faye, it's rude to use a cell phone when someone is talking to you."

"Where are you," Faye quizzed?

"I'm just taking a pee-break at a garage station restaurant." Again a slight untruth. "Oh, Faye, are you there? Are you there? I think we are losing our signal." This was a definite lie. "Look," Grace shouted, "I'll call you tonight when I get checked in. I'll call you. Don't worry."

Grace clicked the telephone off, got up from the bench, and staggered into the bathroom beside the bench. She leaned her forehead against her reflection in the cracked, mildew covered mirror above the grease-stained porcelain sink. A dim light coming through the portal shaped window cast a gray shadow over her already pallor complexion. And then the apple pie and her meager breakfast came out of her in a torrent. She tried to flush the broken handle on the toilet.

• • •

The nurses' aide found Grace's mother on the floor of the washroom, wedged between the toilet and the sink. She'd tried to get to the toilet, they told Grace. Your mother can't remember that she can't walk and her brain isn't telling her legs how to move anymore. We can't be with her twenty-four hours a day.

And from that day on Grace's mother was strapped into her chair and she was made to wear special adult underpants that everyone knew were diapers. And from that day on Grace swore it wouldn't be like that for her.

• • •

The back of the toilet tank lay across the seat as Grace reached into the frigid water to pull the lever and manually flush the toilet. Then without a second thought she laid the cell phone in the bottom of the tank and watched as the water slowly oozed over it. One less clue to help anyone track her down.

Outside, the fickle autumn weather shifted again from sunny to cloudy. A beagle mutt raised its leg and peed against the telephone pole across from where Grace was sitting and then kicked up the dirt and grass before heading off down the road and disappeared into a cornfield.

An older man, well into his eighties with a leathery wrinkled face came over to Grace. He pulled a soiled red hankie out of the back pocket of his oily coveralls and began to wipe his hands.

"How ye tiday? Ye gotch yer car run out of gas up the valley way have ye now. Well, then we can help ye out if ye got the money honey." He tucked the hankie into his back pocket. "Twenty'll do'er fine. Got a gas can waiting for you out front fer when Bobby boy comes back, unless of course he gets waylaid by that sweet, young Chantal. All the boys is hopin' to get way laid by her, if ye knows what I mean." He winked.

• • •

What Grace loved about Jason and Bryan was that she never had to worry about fending off their advances because there just weren't any. And they were both great dance partners, especially Bryan who signed up with Grace for ballroom dancing lessons one winter.

They learned to rumba, foxtrot, cha-cha and jive. Every Thursday evening they danced their hearts out in the high school gymnasium and never went to bed with one another at the end of the night. It was heavenly bliss and Grace beamed like royalty from November to March all that year even though the real queen was Bryan.

For Halloween one year Grace dressed as Colette in men's attire and Bryan was Colette in woman's attire. Jason came as Picasso. They knew how to enjoy life to the fullest.

• • •

The year that Grace's mother slipped away in her morphine induced sleep was the same year that Bryan's ashes were sprinkled all around the base of Eiffel tower. It had been his wish ever since he had been an art student in Paris. It was there in the sixties that he'd met Jason doing portraits of tourists for loose change. He wore a beret and everyone assumed he was from France when he said "merci". The truth was his patois had come down from his mother's side of the family who had worked in a railroad town in northern Ontario. But Bryan had flare. And when Jason first met him sipping espresso at a sidewalk cafe, he was more than intrigued. The two were an instant flame that continued to light up the world until Bryan turned to stardust again.

The year that Grace's mother's life line was finally severed was the same year that Grace was diagnosed with the tumor. It was her secret for months and months until long after her mother had been buried next to her father in the family plot.

She needed to spare Faye the extra worry and in some ways it made it seem untrue or impossible to be happening to her if she just imagined that it wasn't really happening. And for a time Grace almost convinced herself that she had been cured by willing it away. But the will of the cancer was greater than Grace had expected and when the seizures increased she finally had to give in to the truth. She too would be letting go of her life line. She too would one day be released.

33

BY THE TIME Bobby's beat up truck sped away with the empty gas can clanging in the back, the day was more than half spent. Grace sat in the stillness of her car, keys in the ignition, just waiting to decide what to do next.

She knew she would never make it to Quebec before night fall. She'd planned on getting to the outskirts of Gatineau Park where she knew there would be a tourist motel or two to choose from. To find one before sundown meant getting on a major highway, a major highway with more traffic and more chances of getting pulled over by a bored out of his mind police officer parked around some unsuspecting curve in the road, radar gun pointed at the oncoming traffic.

Sleeping in the car at the side of the road would cause suspicion for sure. Stealing into someone's barn would definitely be asking for trouble. Suddenly Grace felt like a fugitive on the run. She rocked her body back and forth, back and forth and smiled.

I am not running away. I am running to.

• • •

Grace was out of breath. She'd run all the way from the woods, across the field to the back door of her parents' house.

"There's a fairy tree. Mommy I saw them. They live in a tree."

Her mother stood stooped over the old wringer washing machine, filling it with a dark load of work pants and plaid shirts. Her mother slowly straightened up and wiped the sweat from her brow with the back of her sleeve. She looked at Grace in a way that without a word being said projected such disdain and hurt that it straightway pierced Grace's delicate universe of believing in all things possible and impossible.

"It's true, Mommy. Come and see. There's a little doorway and acorns all around. They love oak trees Mommy."

"Grace, can't you see I'm busy. Go get your sister."

But Faye was busy too; busy painting her fingernails bright pink and she was certainly not interested in fairies and trees and little girl games. Maybe later, she said. From previous promises of maybe being broken Grace knew that a maybe from Faye meant leave me alone and don't bother me. A maybe meant never.

• • •

The sun was sinking lower and the shadows growing longer. Grace's mind travelled back and forth between the lines on the county roads and the memories of her childhood. The sky was beginning to darken in the west. Soon it would be pitch black and the last thing Grace wanted was to end up driving into the middle of nowhere late at night. And she needed to call Faye to ward off any suspicion.

Ahead was a sign with the symbol of a picnic table on it and an arrow pointing to the right. Grace pulled the car over and it came to a rest below a stand of pine trees. She rolled the windows down and a waft of sweet scented air swept across her face. And on the breeze came the distant sound of a waterfall.

Grace followed the rumbling sound to the edge of the cliff. She leaned over a wooden railing to see the swift water cascading over the rocks in a torrent that seemed to run forever and ever and for a brief moment time vanished into thin air like the mist rising from the water below.

• • •

Life was forever and ever when Grace was small. It was forever into eternity and forever out of eternity. This she knew without anyone telling her. It just was. Sitting on the grass she looked deeply into each blade knowing it had no beginning. If she could go there she would. At night she looked beyond the beyond, past the stars, past the ray of her flashlight that she held pointing toward the big dipper. There is no beginning and there is no end.

• • •

A sudden flap of wings broke into Grace's dream moment. A huge grey heron squawked and flew off to the woods. The last one to leave, thought Grace. The others have long gone.

Back in the car Grace opened the road map and saw that she was only a few miles from a town on the Ottawa River. Surely there would be a road side motel or cabin she could rent for the night. She had enough cash to see her through two days of travelling, eating, and gassing up the car, plus an overnight stay if need be. She had no credit cards. They'd be a dead giveaway, thought Grace. A dead giveaway, she laughed. A dead getaway.

34

SEVERAL OF THE neon lights on the Sleepy Hollow Motel sign were burnt out so that it read "S eepy low tel". Vacancy flashed off and on. Grace drove up beside the green paint-chipped office door. It was barely illuminated by a yellowing overhead bulb covered in spider webs and dangling from it were the dead remnants of flies and moths snagged during the summer months.

Awkwardly Grace got out of the car, stiff from a long day behind the wheel. Her balance was off and she fell against the car door slamming it shut behind her. Straightening up she took a breath and made her way over to the motel door. It was locked.

Grace leaned forward. She could barely see through the grit on the window. There was a small desk. It had plastic flowers in a vase on one side and a rack of tourist brochures on the other. A torn map of Ontario was stapled to the front of the desk. Beyond the reception area was another room. Grace recognized the irregular flashes of light. Someone was watching television but all she could see was a pair of fluffy pink slippers perched on a footstool.

Grace knocked. No answer. She knocked again. Louder.

Finally the slippers landed on the floor and a woman of substantial proportions waddled up to the door and undid the latch.

"Gracious girl. Did you not see the sign? Ring the bell. How long you been standing there? My gawd I was watching my show and I didn't hear you come or nothing. Hate to miss my show. They got these girls trying to scramble over these big balloons and they keep falling in the water. Oh my, it's some funny to watch. Lord knows I should be doing something more useful with my life but the summer was a killer and I just needed a bit of down time so anyway come in come in."

The woman shuffled behind the reception desk and butted out her cigarette in an ashtray that resembled a flattened version of the parliament buildings. She had on a mustard green track suit that must have fit her at one time or another unless it was picked up at the thrift shop. There was a stain on the bosom of the top and her hair was pinned up in a bun that looked like she'd stepped out of a 1960's beach party movie and had forgotten to change with the times. But her smile was generous and Grace felt at ease.

• • •

The nurse at the hospital was brisk. Everything was clinical and impersonal. Get the patients over and done with oozed from her pores and Grace was on the same page. Get this treatment over and done with and get me home. She'd read about people having to undergo radiation. She'd been warned of the side effects but not until it was actually happening to her did she fully appreciate the nausea and horror. Killing cells to save cells. It was hit-and-miss, but it seemed to be the roulette wheel of life and death to play, at the time.

No. Grace did not much care for the nurse and her starchy attitude. And like her mother who had become increasingly outspoken in her later years Grace suggested that perhaps she should find another line of work. Perhaps a mortician would suit her better.

• • •

Motel rooms were never a romantic notion for Grace. She couldn't get it out of her head that hundreds, maybe thousands of couples had copulated inside the four walls. And this room fit the bill. There were cigarette burns embedded in the tan colored carpet, worn threadbare by the footsteps of tired tourists or desperate lovers escaping unhappy marriages in their upstanding communities.

The bathroom light switch worked and when Grace flicked it on a fan whirled and the light buzzed in syncopation. It was clean enough with a tiny bar of soap in a paper wrapping on the sink and three overly washed bleached towels hanging from the rack. The tub smelled like Lysol even though there was rust on the drain and some black mould in the corners.

A crummy brown synthetic cover was neatly tucked around the bed. Grace pulled back the cover and discovered another cigarette burn on the blanket. The sheets were crisp and clean but didn't quite fit. Grace walked to the far side of the bed away from the alarm clock radio. Everyone slept on that side. Everyone, except Grace, who took off her shoes, flopped down on the bed and fell asleep from sheer exhaustion of the day.

• • •

When Grace was little she could fly in her dreams. Her sister couldn't catch her when they played tag. Grace flapped her arms and rose above the telephone wires and up into the branches of the huge elm tree. From there she could see over top of her house and all the way to both ends of the street. And then she'd swoop down and tease her sister to try and catch her again.

• • •

Grace woke with start. There was a sharp rap on the door. At first she wasn't exactly sure of where she was – her home or the hospital or the motel? Finally her senses returned and she sat up, stood for a moment to catch her balance then proceeded to the door. Through the peep-hole Grace could see it was the owner. In the distortion of the glass she looked even more roly-poly not unlike an animated television character.

"You left your car lights on." She shouted through the shut door.

Grace cracked the door open as far as the safety latch allowed. "Thanks." And she closed the door.

The alarm clock radio flashed to 7:35. Grace knew that Faye would be pacing a rut in the rug. She had to phone her sister to prevent her from doing anything stupid or rash, like calling the cops. But first things first. Go out to the car and turn off the lights before the battery dies.

35

THE TELEPHONE BOOTH oozed from years of over use. Grace squeezed through the plastic swing doors. They bore witness to the teenage lovers who had carved their names with a sharp blade beside the profanities of perverts making random obscene phone calls. The phone book holder dangled from a broken chain with only a few of the ripped yellow pages remaining. Someone had smeared gum on top of the operator information on the front of the pay phone itself.

    Cautiously Grace lifted the receiver as if holding up a dead fish. The filth made her stomach flip. But she had no choice. The motel rooms didn't have phones in them and she had to call Faye who would be imagining the worst of worst scenarios, calling every five minutes to a dead cell phone that lay beneath a gallon of water in the back of a toilet tank over a hundred kilometers to the south.

    Grace pushed the zero keypad and a prerecorded voice gave Grace too many options to choose from, none of which made any sense so she didn't push any of the other buttons. After all of the instructions had been completed without a response from Grace – a real person spoke - first in French and then in English. Finally. The operator made the collect call.

• • •

The world swung upside down. Grace flipped her body backwards through the worn out tire that her father had hung from the branch of the sturdy oak behind the house. The ground became up and the sky became below. Up and below. Up and below. Grace giggled with delight, her curly red hair swishing back and forth. The tree was dangling its branches down toward the cloudy floor of her planet. At five years of age Grace was the master of this gleeful absurdity and it tickled her desire to control the order of her world.

• • •

"Where in the world are you?" Faye's first words did not surprise Grace.

"Where do you think I am?"

Grace did not want to lie if she could avoid it. "I know I am late but everything is fine. Yes, yes, I understand you've been calling. Yes, yes…."

Grace could not get a word in as Faye ranted about how she had been calling for hours and there had been no answer on the cell phone. Grace thought of saying there weren't any transmitters in the area which might have been the case but decide to tell a half truth.

"I left it at a gas station."

"You what!"

Grace assured Faye that the resort was everything that she had expected it would be. That, yes, it was clean and no, there weren't any weirdoes in the lobby, and yes there was a lovely restaurant. And finally, after much reassuring, Faye and Grace said goodnight.

Grace listened to the hum of the phone after Faye had long hung up at her end. For several minutes she stood motionless as if in suspended animation. Grace realized she would miss her sister's constant nagging and worrying. She would miss that peculiar love that she had always felt from Faye. And the guilt of never calling her again suddenly caused Grace to break out in sobs. Grace sank to her knees in the cradled confines of the smudged telephone booth at the end of the driveway leading to the motel.

• • •

The tree fort was their secret. No one would know about it, not even Faye. Kevin and Grace swore on it that summer.

They found all these bits of broken lumber stashed out back of the train station when they tore it down to make way for the brick one that was being built. Kevin sort of borrowed his father's hammer and buck saw when he was at work at the Milk Plant. Together, Grace and Kevin had gone scrounging along the ditches for old pop and beer bottles to cash in. It wasn't long before they had enough money to buy nails at Saunders Hardware Store next to the IGA up on the main highway.

Beyond the back fields stood a row of trees marking of the old boundaries of the farmers' fields and a small grove of trees that felt like a medieval hideaway. Grace never told Kevin that she was pretending to be Maid Marion. He was three years older and had more practical things in mind - like how to build a floor between the branches and how to make a wall and a roof.

All that summer whenever they could they worked on their fort and by the time September rolled around they had a complete floor and one wall with a window cut right into it. Then school started and things changed.

It was on one of those warm autumn Sundays in early October that they decided to put the nails in an old du Maurier tobacco tin and hide it in a knoll in the elm tree. They'd finish their fort next summer. They promised.

Kevin moved on to high school and Grace went into grade six. Grace wondered why he slicked his hair back with some kind of smelly cream and then she noticed that he was hanging out with girls in tight sweaters. Grace watched him carry their books home from school. He'd laugh and wink at Grace and she was sure it was because of their secret tree fort.

But by the time June came around Kevin had picked up a summer job working with his Dad at the Milk Plant and Grace was left to look after the fort. She pulled out the tobacco tin and discovered that the winter had turned every nail into rust and the dream of building the tree fort was a dream that had turned to dust.

• • •

Grace knew she was dreaming. She knew she was lying on the bed in the motel room but she was also flying. She felt herself leave her body and swoop through the crack in the window she'd left open before turning off the light. The stale stank air of the room clung to everything and she had decided it was better to be a bit chilly than stuffed up.

In her dream she was hovering over a swaying pine tree and sitting in its branches were her mother and her father, and reaching to catch her lest she fall, was David.

36

THE CHILL OF the autumn morning penetrated the room. Grace was unaware of the deer standing on the frost covered lawn outside the motel room window. Nor did she hear the distant calling of the geese flying across the scarlet tinted sky of the eastern sunrise. With her head buried beneath the pillows she lay in fetal position, the synthetic blankets barely keeping her warm.

The decision to not put on the heater in the room was not a conscious one. It just was. And what finally woke her was the demanding urge to relieve her bladder. Surfacing from her dream world Grace was met with the dank, musty smell of the room and an abrupt awareness of how frigging cold it really was. Pissing into the toilet Grace felt the warmth ooze from her body. Then a shiver raced from her toes to her hair roots. The journey must go on, she thought. The journey must go on.

• • •

The first time Grace peed outside was when she was four. They'd all been swimming at the lake and she had to go so bad it ached. Her mother had told her not to do it in the lake so Grace waded up onto the shore, stepped out of her bathing suit, and let the warm trickle race down her legs onto the pebbled beach. There was a roar of laughter from her father and her uncle and then her mother threw a towel around her and scolded her for not going to the stinky out house on the other side of the park.

Then when Grace was seven Kevin dared her to do it out behind the abandoned chicken hut in the farmer's field across the road from where they lived. He said she could ride his "two wheeler" if she did it. Grace told him she would do it but he couldn't look. Kevin agreed. Grace slid her blue shorts and underpants with the pink and yellow butterflies on them down to her ankles while Kevin turned his back but just as she started to make the puddle Kevin turned and stared right at her. Grace screamed. Kevin jumped on his bike and peddled away like lightning.

• • •

The golden sun broke through the early morning haze that lay just beyond the hotel room window. Grace stood staring out at the maple covered hills on the far side of the river. Hues of red, orange and yellow swept across a landscape canvas. The play of light upon dark danced before her eyes. Grace imagined how she might paint it; how she would capture the mystery of the rising mist and the warming of the morning sun; how each tree was distinct and separate, yet together they were one harmonious explosion of color.

A flittering flock of chickadees scooted from bush to bush. The season was quickly changing. All the signs were there. Grace sighed. This was her favorite time of the year. And this was a perfect day.

Grace turned to look back into the room where the bed lay in a jumble of sheets and blankets. Her brown overnight bag sat perched open on the one and only chair in the room and her shoes were at the door. Time for a shower, she thought, then hit the road.

• • •

David did most of the driving that summer but every now and again for those long stretches across Manitoba and Saskatchewan Grace took over the wheel while David curled up on the back seat and fell asleep. They lived for the day. And though they never said it in words they believed they would live forever – and they did for the whole of their short time together.

The trip was speckled with a flat tire and two close calls, both with transport trucks. At night they camped at the side of the road and pulled over to relieve themselves whenever and wherever they felt like it as long as it was in the country. Towns meant looking for a garage bathroom or one in a diner when they felt they could afford to buy a treat, like homemade apple pie or a fresh bag of cheese curds.

The journey wasn't so much about the miles on the odometer as it was about the number of times they made love to one another under the stars and the way that David teased Grace until she giggled like a school girl. It was a journey of love.

• • •

The steaming warmth from the shower caressed Grace's body. She tilted her head back so that the water rushed gently over her face. Then she adjusted the shower head, turned around and let the pelting water massage her shoulders. Grace released a sigh of great relief and gave silent thanks for that moment, free of any worry, free of any demands, free of any constraints.

Without warning the bathtub began to rise up and fall like a ship tossed on the sea. Grace grabbed the shower curtain and held on for dear life until at last the motion subsided. The tumor had not gone away. It would never go away. But I will, thought Grace, I will go away.

• • •

THE TRUTH ABOUT TREES

The day that Grace left to go to Art College her mother had a check list the length of her arm. Did she have toothpaste? Yes Mom. Did she forget to pack her sewing kit? No, Mom.

Next came the "be careful" suggestions. Don't forget to call when you get there? Yes Mom. And don't go out alone after dark. Yes, Mom. It's a big city Grace and there's a lot of crime in that city and you never know what could happen in the dark. Yes. Mom, I know what to do.

Grace could hardly wait to get going. That morning she'd already filled up the trunk and backseat of the Buick with her suitcase, bedding and books. Leaving the hometown was easy for girl who saw things they way that Grace did. Anyone who stayed behind ended up working in a factory or getting pregnant and unlike Faye, that was not a destiny that Grace was willing to be a part of.

Her father sat at the wheel, a cigarette hanging from his mouth, fingers drumming on the dashboard. Grace hugged her mother one more time then climbed onto the passenger seat and shut the door. Her father started to drive away. Grace turned to wave goodbye - but her mother didn't see. She was wiping the tears from her eyes as she walked toward the house and disappeared behind the dust kicked up by the tires spinning out of the driveway.

• • •

Grace put on the same clothes she had on the day before. She grabbed her overnight bag, her purse and the keys to the car. With one last look around the room Grace opened the door and stepped into the fresh air of the crisp October morning.

37

"**WILL THAT BE** cash or credit?"

The owner of the motel butted her cigarette out on the clock tower of the parliament buildings ash tray. She was wearing the same leisure outfit, the same fluffy slippers and the same smile with bright orange lipstick. Her hair was rolled up in curlers and she had a yellow chiffon scarf holding them altogether – a scarf that resembled something Grace's mother once bought at the Woolworths. That was the day Grace spent her piggy bank savings on her first fish bowl and filled it full of shimmering guppies.

"Cash or credit sweetheart?"

Grace realized she was staring at the woman's hair do.

"Oh this? There's a baby shower for my cousin's daughter this afternoon. Can't say I'm too thrilled about it. It's her fifth kid and Lord knows why we have to go through this every time. It isn't like there aren't enough hand-me-downs, if you know what I mean. Oh well, you can choose your friends but you can't choose your family."

Grace put the cash on the counter.

"So where you off to? Nice day for a drive, eh?"

Grace smiled. "I'm heading north."

"North, eh? There're some beautiful leaves still on the trees this year. Not like others. Most years they're long gone. Could happen overnight. You never know. Snow could come too. Just like that. No warning. No nothing. Anyways today's good. Wish I were going with you but I'm tied up here now on account of Frank, my husband, he's driving rig for the lumber company and they're ain't nobody here but us chickens to do mind the desk and do all the clean up too.

The season's over and the girl I had doing the rooms has gone back to school. Lot of good that'll do her. North, eh. Watch out for the Moose. If you see one, get out of its way quick. They'll charge your car faster than a freight train. You take care now honey. Have a nice time. And come again."

Grace smiled as she pushed the door open. "Thanks," she said. "Thanks." The door creaked to a close behind Grace and the gravel on the drive crunched beneath her shoes.

• • •

Sometimes on the Saturday after payday Grace's whole family went to the Woolworths store on the main street. It had everything anyone would want - from underwear to fountain pens. There was a snack bar on one side where for ten cents you could have a plate of fries and for another nickel you could have gravy on top. The smell of deep frying grease permeated everything.

In the back corner was the pet department where multicolored budgies hopped from post to post all chirping and squawking, the bottom of the cages covered in their white droppings. Beside the birds were the aquariums full of exotic iridescent fish with unpronounceable names. This was Grace's favorite place to go.

One summer before grade five Grace had saved all of her chore money for a trip to the store. Together Grace and Faye tore down the street ahead of their parents. They stepped on the rubber pad, the automatic door swung open, and the smell of potatoes boiling in the fryer filled their nostrils.

Faye beetled it over to the cosmetic counter looking for the palest possible lipstick she could find while Grace's mother went in search of a new Gothic bra and spatula to replace the one that had melted on the burner the other week. Grace's father marched directly over to the snack bar where a waitress chewing gum took his order for a double-double. Grace saw her father wink at the girl in the uniform that was hemmed so high that when she bent over to get the mugs from the bottom shelf you could see her underwear.

It seemed a bit weird at the time and Grace didn't really know why because she had other things on her mind. Guppies.

• • •

The morning frost on the car windows was as thick as icing on a cake. Grace looked in the back seat for the scraper but it wasn't there. She'd forgotten to take it from the garage. Great help that is, she thought. Grace rifled though her purse hoping to find something, anything. A credit card would have worked but she left them all at home so no one would know her identity.

Damn it, damn it, double damn it. Grace threw her hands up in the air. The rap on the window had made her just about jump out of her skin.

"Here you go sweetie!" It was the woman from the motel wielding a scraper in her hand. "I see you haven't come too prepared for the north, have you? Here take this one. Frank, he gets them from all across the country. Souvenirs. He'll never miss it; he's already got three from this place anyway."

Grace thanked the woman who handed her the blue scrapper with the logo for a tow truck and the words 'Tommy's Garage, Sparks and Plugs, Sudbury' printed on it.

"You don't look too good." The woman seemed concerned. "You okay?"

"Oh yeah," said Grace. "I'm fine. Guess I need some breakfast."

"Well that's easy. Two miles up the road there's a trucker stop. They make the best dog gone western omelet around. Tell them Shirley sent you and they'll give you extra home fires. Good then. Jeez it's cold. Well good luck."

• • •

"That'll be one dollar for the guppies, two for the bowl and fifty-nine cents for the fish food."

The cashier wore a fuzzy angora sweater over her starched blue uniform. She had on cat rimmed glasses and hair that was teased up into a place where wasps might make a nest in an urban legend sort of way. The cashier took Grace's change with her pointy painted fingernails and dropped the coins into the penny, nickel and dime slots of the register feigning an attitude that said you're wasting my time kid. Grace smiled. She had six guppies to take home. Six beautiful guppies.

Next at the cash was Faye. She placed two tubes of lipstick on the conveyor belt – Cherry Blossom Pink and Pearly Secrets. Grace's mother had a new white Gothic bra, a pair of nylon stockings, a box of Kotex, a yellow chiffon scarf, and one spanking new spatula. Grace's father had a smirk on his face.

Everyone got what they wanted thought Grace - especially Grace who carried her plastic bag full of shining guppies out to the sparkling sunlight streaming down on the main drag.

38

SUNLIGHT STREAMED ONTO the dashboard of the car. Grace could see that it was going to be a beautiful day. The sky was baby powder blue and the rays from the sun glistened on the frost still clinging to the mown hay in the farmers' fields. Diamonds in the rough, thought Grace.

Driving the car along the curving country road that ran parallel to the Ottawa River, Grace felt a sense of freedom and abandonment well up inside and it filled her with an excitement that she hadn't experienced in years. This she would miss, the being one with her car, just driving through the country side for no special reason except to get away from life for a while. For a while, she thought. And then forever.

• • •

Not long after Grace moved back to the hometown she bought her first car - a used Volvo with a stick shift, a loose front bumper and lots of wear and tear on the upholstery. It got Grace from point A to point B and came in handy for those occasional trips to the hardware store and the local flea markets.

Most weekends Grace took her mother for short jaunts about the countryside, to the favorite spots like the gravel pit where her mother went swimming as a kid or to the park with the gazebo. Your father proposed to me there, she'd say every time they drove by. Once they went to the cemetery to see where Grace's father had been buried but that made her mother agitated and confused so Grace stopped going there. Even when her mother asked her to take her there Grace would find an excuse not to do it. Sometimes they would go for ice cream. Sometimes Grace said they were running out of gas.

• • •

A monolithic sized trucker sign suddenly appeared on the horizon. There was no missing it. It dominated everything in every direction; even the row of hydro towers seemed dwarfed by it. Rotating in slow motion circles was an enormous three dimensional coffee mug. It hung over a sign with big orange letters on a yellow background that read - Pay at the Pump - Open 24 Hours - Coffee. Coffee? Good idea, thought Grace. Good idea.

• • •

On the occasional weekend when Faye agreed to look after their mother and Grace wasn't tied up with her teaching responsibilities at the college she'd bundle up the easel, some canvases, her watercolors and brushes and drive out to one of the little villages that dotted the length of the canal. She'd pack a lunch of fresh baked rolls, a chunk of cheese, celery sticks, an apple and a thermos of dark Columbian coffee with lots of sweet carnation milk to see her through the day.
  Her favorite spot was down a long dirt road. There was a huge willow tree half hanging over the river providing Grace with a shady canopy where she could set up her folding chair and paint her impressions of the

old stone mill. And on days such as these all time disappeared – no seconds, no minutes, no hours – no need to do anything but be dazzled by the light dancing on the leaves, and mesmerized by the blending of the silver grey blue black rhythms of the water.

• • •

The sight of the enormous gas station parking lot overwhelmed Grace. Lined up like dominoes was a long row of semis, rigs and tractor trailers. She noticed that the gas station was sandwiched between the old highway that she had been driving on and an interchange leading on and off the provincial highway. Then she spotted them - two police cruisers parked next to one another only a few feet from the doors that led to the restaurant.

Grace glanced over and saw that the cop cars were empty. There was no way she could risk going inside or stopping for that matter. If they made a mental note of her appearance they might be able to trace her later on and if they checked the plates it definitely would put an end to her plan.

Without hesitation, without even looking around, Grace drove by the cruisers; past the gas pumps and right around the back end of the restaurant until the tires of her car hit the dirt of a back road. Grace stepped on the gas pedal. The car fishtailed its way beyond the shadows of the gigantic trucker sign. Grace threw her head back and let out a yahoo - look out Bonnie and Clyde – I'm hell bent fer gittin outta here.

• • •

"You want to know why this car is here."

Kevin was sitting in the front seat of the rusting old Ford that had seen better days before the war. The back doors had been ripped off their hinges and almost all the windows were smashed in. Grace stood outside in the long grass leaning on a nearly dead tree beside the car. She stared at Kevin.

"I know why that car is here." Grace didn't actually know but she didn't want Kevin to think she was stupid or something.

"Why then?"

Grace had to come up with something. "It's, it's just old that's all. It just isn't any good anymore and there're new ones and ..."

"It's because old man McAffery came out here and gassed himself in it on account his wife left him for some guy who came back from the war. Thought he was dead but no, he shows up and she runs off with him. So the old man done himself in."

"Did himself in." Grace didn't correct Kevin all the time but today he was getting on her nerves.

"That's what I said. Right here on this seat. Police found him a week later and the bugs and worms were eating him up. But one of his hands fell off. See."

Kevin threw a bone at Grace. Grace screamed and took off across the field like a jack rabbit out running a fox. It was only when they got back at her front porch that Kevin caught up with her and laughed. "It's only a chicken bone. Scaredy-cat."

Grace was some perturbed with Kevin. So much so that she didn't speak to him for a week but one day on the way to school she finally asked. "Was that true? Did old man McAffery kill himself?"

Kevin just looked at Grace and said. "That's what I heard."

39

IT WASN'T LONG before the weather changed. Unpredictable fickle fall weather, thought Grace.

Drizzle splattered onto the dust covered windshield. Grace flicked on the wipers. It was too soon. The blades made an arched smudge across her vision. Grace hit the button for the washer fluid and one tiny spit barely spurted out. With each swish of the blades it got worse. Slowly Grace geared down to reduce the speed, and when she checked the rear-view mirror to make sure no one was behind her all she could see was a thick film of wet dirt kicked up from her frantic gangster like getaway.

God, this is not how I planned it. I do not want to drive into the ditch or be rear-ended by someone.

A knot tightened in Grace's gut. She rolled down the window just in time to see a flagman in an orange vest frantically waving at her to pull to the right and make way for the on-coming traffic.

A four by four hauling a mobile home half the size of a barn drove past and splashed up a ton of mud headed straight for the window that Grace had managed to close just in time. Following the late weather campers was a delivery van, a compact red hatchback, and holding up the rear was a huge empty school bus probably going back to the driver's home until pick up time.

The next thing Grace knew there was another man in an orange safety vest rapping at the window on the passenger side. Grace leaned over and rolled it down.

"Got a bucket full of water from the creek below this bridge we're fixin'. Thought you might want me to throw it on the windshield there on a count you can't see shit through it. Ain't ya got no washer fluid?"

Grace called out to him. "Ran out a few miles back."

"Well there's a station in the village if you take a right at the next intersection and follow it straight for about five or six miles give or take. Have a g'day."

And with that he threw the water on the windshield and Grace flicked the wiper switch. She could see the flag man waving her to move ahead. As she passed by, he grinned and tipped his hard hat as if to say, "It takes all kinds."

• • •

The yellow school bus was full of giggling grade eight girls and teasing grade eight boys. Every window was open. Grace felt the warm spring air blow down the front of her cotton blouse with the made in China cartoon version of the Beatles stenciled on the back. She'd picked it out at the Zellers especially for this trip. It was tree planting day and Grace had been looking forward to the prospect of being teamed up with Richard who at thirteen already had hair on his chin. And he played the drums or at least he claimed to play the drums and he was constantly getting told to sit in the hall because he drummed his pencils on the desk.

Grace wasn't sure why it felt so exciting to stand next to him. They rarely even spoke but when they did Grace got all clammy and said stupid things like wasn't it cool how their teacher could see out of the back of her head. Richard would smile and then walk away but now their names had been put together to pair up as tree planting partners.

Grace sat near the front of the bus with Joan who had this annoying habit of smacking her juicy fruit gum. And Richard sat slumped in the middle of the back seat, his long legs splayed open. Grace looked back and caught him winking at her. The shiver ran from the back of her neck to her spine.

• • •

Grace turned right at the first intersection, just as the man had suggested, and followed it until she came to a hamlet that was nothing more than a cross roads with a run-down gas station on one corner and a red brick two storey house sitting kitty corner to it. The building looked like it might have seen a more prosperous time long ago but now it had every manner of broken appliance lined up in the yard - old chairs, bits of machinery and a huge weatherworn sign claiming there were antiques for sale. At the side was a shed with a mongrel dog tied up with a chain. It looked like it had been trained to be mean or maybe it was just crazy from being kept tied up all the time. Grace was not about to go anywhere near it and find out.

As Grace swung into the gas station she could see that there was a stash of washer fluid beside a pump bearing a crooked sign that read out of order. The guy was right. There was washer fluid for sale. Good thing I don't need gas, Grace muttered to herself. Still she turned off the ignition so that she didn't waste what was in the tank. Grace grabbed her purse and rolled the window down. A teenage boy with pop bottle thick glasses stepped out of the garage, wiping his greasy hands on a well used rag.

"Can I help you ma'am?"

"Just some washer fluid please."

Grace sat in silence as the young man opened the hood of the car and poured the fluid from the plastic container. He let the hood drop down with such force that Grace jumped in the driver's seat.

"That'll be four fifty plus tax."

Grace handed him a five dollar bill. "How's that?"

"Dunno. Gotta add it up on the machine."

Grace rifled around in her purse. "Here's four quarters. That'll do, I'm sure. If not, you can keep the change."

"But, but, but... "

"It's you're lucky day."

Grace put the car into gear and drove back onto road. Gazing over her left shoulder she could see that the boy was still looking at the money in his hands. For a brief moment Grace wondered how long it would take for the grease covered boy to figure out what had just happened.

• • •

Richard handed the shovel to Grace.

"You dig and I'll plant."

Grace stood stunned. All the other boys were digging and the girls were planting.

"Just kidding," said Richard. "Here, give it over. I'll dig."

"No, I can do it." Grace was not about to show she was like all the other girls. "I'm not a wimp you know." Then she realized that Richard might be embarrassed that he was planting like the girls were.

"Tell you what. Let's do the handle of the rake like we do for baseball. Whoever gets to the top gets to dig." Grace tossed it to Richard who caught it midway to the tip.

Hand over hand they touched each other. Sometimes Grace just used her fingers and sometimes her whole hand stretched from baby finger to thumb. And when she could see that Richard was about to lose, she opted not to beat him. She left enough room for him to conquer her. It was a fine game of flirtation.

All that morning they planted trees and unlike all the other partners, Richard and Grace took turns planting and digging. By noon they had put in over thirty trees and had learned a lot about each other. They *learned more in two hours than they had in all of the years since Richard came to the school in grade six.*

They talked about fishing and bowling and shooting stars. Grace said she wanted to be an anthropologist and Richard said he was going to join the army like his Dad – like his Dad who was never around anymore. He was going to see the world one day. "Me too," said Grace.

By grade nine Grace had taken up art classes and she knew that being an anthropologist was merely a phase. She never saw Richard after that spring. He moved away. But Grace heard that he got busted for dealing marijuana and was sent to a reform school up back of the Rideau.

Still Grace longed for the feeling that she got when Richard teased her and touched her on the tree planting trip. It made her feel wobbly and wonderful and she wondered if it would ever happen again, that delirious sensation.

V

I hear the wind among the trees
Playing the celestial symphonies;
I see the branches downward bent,
Like keys of some great instrument.

~Henry Wadsworth Longfellow

40

THE LEAVES ON the birch trees quivered in the morning breeze. Grace sat shivering in the line-up of cars waiting for the ferry to take them across the Ottawa River to Quebec. She'd turned the engine off, unlike the people in front of her, their cars spewing out exhaust as they sat with the heaters turned up. Grace knew she had to ration the gas. Her cash would only go so far and she still had a few more things to get.

On the far side of the river the sun broke through the clouds cascading streams of light around the silver spire of the Catholic Church. It dominates the landscape; it consumes the souls of its parishioners, thought Grace. It seemed as if the shadowy secrets of people's lives were entombed in the memory of the stone façade - baptisms, weddings, funerals, the affairs of choir masters and the unwanted touching of lonely-hearted priests. These were the deep secrets of the faithful and the restless.

Grace had a belief in God, but not in the church way. That had long ago disappeared with the days of her disastrous confirmation. God was the ocean reaching out to the sunset. God was the tear in a newborn's eyes. God was a knowing that only sometimes paid a visit like when David held her and rocked her in his arms on those blue black mood swing days that haunted her before her period. God was the unpredictable constant. She knew that God was her reason for being and her support for going.

• • •

The Buddhist monk stood on deck looking back at the B.C. Ferry Terminal. Grace couldn't help but notice his orange flowing robes in the sea of hippies and retired couples with matching outfits. She was on her way to see an exhibit of Emily Carr's paintings in a gallery down on Granville Island.

Grace quietly stood beside the monk. His presence intrigued her. She had read about Buddhism, how to some it was a religion, to others a way of life, and that in many ways it seemed to mirror the teachings she could recall from her daydreaming times at Sunday school – forgiveness, patience, compassion. Then he spoke.

"Your trees. Your trees are the libraries of years long past. Do you not think so? They hold all the history of our planet, since the beginning of time."

Grace smiled. This was more than a coincidence. This was a meant to be. She was well aware of the spiritual element in the tree paintings of Emily Carr and here this monk with the bald head wanted to talk about the spirit within trees.

He reached into his pocket and pulled out a folded piece of linen. He handed it to Grace.

Grace carefully unfolded the cloth and discovered that it was wrapped around a leaf – a leaf she had never seen before.

"It is Gingko. It comes from the garden in our monastery near Hiroshima. The gingko tree has survived unchanged since the Jurassic period. It even survived the bombing of our city."

Grace gestured to give it back.

"No, you keep it. You be like the tree – strong and wise."

He turned to walk away.

"Now I go to see where we are going. But you know we are only right here." And then he laughed.

• • •

The Ottawa River Ferry swooped up to the dock sending the smell of its diesel into the air. There was a crash of the gate opening up and then the cars from Quebec drove up the hill past the line-up that Grace was in.

The ferry man gestured for Grace to proceed toward the left. For a moment Grace had a little inside joke. Could this man with the unshaven beard and grubby coveralls be the ferry man on the River Styx? Don't look back. You'll turn to stone.

"Seven fifty," he said in a French accent. Grace had the change ready and she dropped it into his stained muscular hand.

"You be careful on de odder side. Plenty of pot ole on de roads between 'ere and de next town."

Grace realized that he knew she was not a regular. She hoped he hadn't taken too close a look.

• • •

For one summer Grace and David lived on a house boat near Skidigate. It was cozy and compact. There was a small propane stove in one corner next to a makeshift galley kitchen where Grace cooked up red snapper stew most weekends and the living space had a built in sofa that became the bed at night. The gentle rocking motion of the waves was soothing and making love with David to the movement was ever so erotic and safe. But it was those storms blowing in from the ocean that made Grace want to put her feet back on dry land. That's when they returned to their house up on Hippie Hill. That autumn David added a studio onto their house and Grace took to her painting with an unending passion.

• • •

The water on the Ottawa River was exceptionally calm and Grace was thankful for that. She stood next to the railing. Several signs were wired onto the iron mesh, advertising county fairs, plumbers, and house insurance agents. Grace noticed the huge one for the Giant Tiger Department Store. Maybe she could get her supplies there.

The ferry seemed to glide effortlessly across the water. A huge heron took flight and croaked out its dismay. But the seagulls stood their ground on an island of sandy silt that had accumulated at the mouth of a creek just where it emptied into the river. A few of the gulls took turns swooping up and around but most of them huddled together getting ready to depart. Grace smiled. Soon the summer birds would all be gone.

Back in the car Grace started the engine on cue and drove up the corrugated metal ramp and onto the road that went past the church and its graveyard on the left. On the right was an aging fairground that might once have sparkled with newness and excitement. The shadowy hint of English words was still legible. Someone had painted over them with white wash in case the language police didn't approve of it. Grace made out the words - Country Music Jamboree Every Weekend.

At the stop sign Grace took a left and pulled up beside the Irish Pub and stared at the brick wall mural full of leaping leprechauns. This was the valley - a place where the Irish, Scots and French worked side by side in the lumber mills. Where men died and ballads were born.

Grace remembered the story her mother had told her about her own grandfather who in the 1870's had settled up near Renfrew and how in those days the land had been covered with the great white pine. How the Prince of Wales had come to visit and all the pomp and circumstance that had taken place. People talked about it for years.

41

NOT SINCE MAKING her decision had Grace felt sorry for herself. She felt sorry for Faye who she prayed would understand. Death was the one thing everyone knew was for certain. And Grace was not going to put Faye through the agony of watching her wither away. It would be worse than her never knowing where she had chosen to die. No, Grace did not feel sorry for herself.

Grace was hungry. The window on the front of the Irish Pub had an all day breakfast sign on one of those plastic boards the letters slide onto it. The letter "k" was falling off so it read brea_fast. The price was right- $4.95 including coffee. Perfect, thought Grace. This is likely going to be my last meal…the Last Breakfast, Amen.

• • •

Grace's father stood proud beside the Coleman stove on the paint chipped picnic table next to the tent that they had all slept in the night before – Faye and Grace on one side and their parents on the other. The smell of bacon made Grace's mouth water. Her father was frying up a storm and he had a pot full of brown beans to go along with it. But the odor had somehow caused Grace's mother to go behind a spruce tree and vomit. Faye called her father and Grace watched the whole thing unfold in slow motion.

"Jeezus, not again. We can't afford another baby. Ah for Christ sake. That's it. We're packing up. We're going home."

"But the bacon," asked Grace.

"Damn the bacon." Grace's father picked up the pan and hurled the whole thing bacon and all into the woods.

On the way back south from the Provincial Park no one said a word, not even Grace's mother who usually talked non-stop. It was a bad day, a really bad day that Grace kept etched in her heart like acid for years to come.

• • •

The inside of the Irish Pub reeked of left over smoke from the night before. It was dim and dank and Grace thought of turning around and leaving until a woman with bleached blond hair, a low cut t-shirt and jeans two sizes too small spoke to her in French.

Grace tried to use her high school French to ask for breakfast and the waitress quickly switched to broken English which was a lot better than Grace's broken French.

"Oh you wantsa dining room. Right tiss way. You don't wantsa stay in eer. It for de old boys, you know what I mean? Dey come round eer in de morning for de beer, savez, but I tell dem dey gotsta wait for de noonhower. So you know what dey do? Deey stay glued to de, how you say, bar stool? But de wifes, dey comes and drag dem home. No. No good for you. You come wid me to de dining room. Bon."

• • •

For close to two weeks Grace and Faye heard their mother throwing up in the bathroom.

"Do you have to puke a baby?" Grace was only six.

"No silly. It's morning sickness." Faye was all of four years older and so much wiser. *"Baby's come from down here."* Grace looked at where Faye was pointing.

"Where you pooh and pee?" Grace frowned. *"No, not where you pooh and pee?"*

The debate went on for several days long after the morning sickness had left. Grace figured the baby would come any day and finally she asked her mother where was the baby going to come from and when could she see it?

There's not going to be a baby Gracie. God took care of that.

And then Grace saw the black circles under her mother's eyes and she thought God had a strange way of loving his little children – giving them and taking them away like that. God was mean.

• • •

The restaurant was painted burnt orange, the color of pumpkins mixed with eggplants. Even the 1960's ceiling tiles had been painted over and the floor looked like it had had a recent beige paint job right on top of the bumpy, old linoleum. Some of the paint was splashed up against the bottoms of the booths. The tables boasted floral fabric cloths with matching burnt orange blossoms that lay under a protective plastic table cloth for easy cleaning.

On her right, a couple of women about Grace's age sat laughing and looking at baby pictures. Grandchildren, thought Grace. On the other side three younger men wearing rubber boots were feasting on plates full of eggs, bacon, beans and home-fries.

The waitress took Grace's order. "Over-easy?"

"Sure. Merci."

Grace pulled out her map of the region. She wasn't too sure of the roads. Some years ago she and a friend from the Art College had gone up this way to check out an artists' colony somewhere in the Gatineau. They found it. And they found the tequila - but not the worm. That was a joke, wasn't it? Grace was sure of that as much as she could be sure of anything with all the marijuana they smoked back then.

The waitress appeared out of nowhere carrying a plate full of breakfast big enough to feed a family of five. "Where you goin?"

Grace was startled out of her daydream and definitely not prepared to give an answer.

"Nowhere."

"What you mean you goin nowhere. You got de map out. Everybody got to be goin somewhere. Like I should be going to de Mexico dis winter but you know my boyfriend says we got to go hice fishing. Big fuckin deal. I tell him you go hice fishing. I'm going to a nice hot beach. Life's a beach, no?" She laughed at her own well-worn joke. "So where you goin?"

"Looking for my family history."

"Oh you got de family up eer?"

"Well a long time ago." Grace was not happy about building up this lie. Sure her great grandfather was from the valley but from the Ontario side of the river. Why couldn't she just say, I'm looking for a nice secluded spot where I can go, lay down, and die.

"Oh yeah? What de family name? Maybe I know dem."

Grace was not prepared for this overly affected enthusiasm. She did not want to be noticed. Grace looked at her watch and pulled out the oldest trick in the book.

"Oh my, look at the time. I'll just eat up and get going. Do you know where I can find a place that sells camping equipment?"

"You goin campin? You don't look like de campin kinda fille - woman. Now, my boyfriend, he take you campin sep for I kill 'im first." She placed the bill beside the grease covered napkin holder. "Dere's a place two blocks up dis way. No can miss. Dey got dis stuffed moose head in de window. Called Bulls Eye Sports." And then she hollered to the back, "Quesque dit le mot pour bulls eye?"

42

THE MOUNTED MOOSE head stared down at Grace through a pair of oversized yellow clown-like glasses. Hanging from its neck was a sign, Bulls Eye Sports – Guns, Ammo, Camping Gear, Worms. How the language police missed this one was a curiosity, thought Grace.

Inside were stacks and stacks of hunters' clothing – camouflage coats and pants, piles of toques, grey work socks, and below, lined up neatly on the floor was a row of heavy duty boots. On one wall all manner of outdoor cooking utensils were hung up on hooks sticking out of a utility board. On a shelf behind a glass counter were dozens of rifles and knives with jagged blades.

This was a man's store, the kind of man Grace remembered seeing in old beer commercials and cigarette ads, the kind of man she really didn't understand or care to for that matter. The cramped confusion of the store weighed heavily on Grace. Her palms began to perspire as a sudden surge of mixed emotions combined with a confusing moral dilemma overtook her state of mind and whole physical well being.

Okay, so maybe it's alright to kill what you eat. Maybe if you kill it and then eat it you at least know it isn't something that you ordered at a takeout window of a fast food chain. It isn't like you're eating beef that's destroying the rain forest. Or was it an innocent animal, lured and caught for the thrill of the kill? Grace was feeling more and more conflicted and was about to leave when a man as short as he was wide appeared out of the back room and asked if he could be of some assistance.

"Yes, no, maybe, I think so." Grace's inner voice shouted, come on get it together. "Sleeping bag? Do you carry winterized sleeping bags?"

• • •

For several weeks after the accident tore David from her heart Grace curled up at night in his down filled sleeping bag, the one he often took with him for the long protests at the logging sites. She engulfed herself in the sweet scent of burnt cedar, the smell he carried in his long black hair when he came back to their home on Hippie Hill.

Her dreams were ethereal and vivid as if she could leave her body behind and never return. Once she was standing beside a tree covered in thousands of brilliant fluttering monarch butterflies. And on another night she saw herself stirring embers in a fire and as each spark rose higher into the night sky a new star was born until the whole of her heaven was filled with a shimmering, dazzling light.

The sleeping bag went with Grace to Toronto where in the middle of the freezing winter she used it as a comforter on her bed. Again the dreams took her on incredible journeys, beautiful and terrifying, grotesque and confusing. One dream came back again and again.

She was lost in a huge cemetery filled with towering Celtic crosses and giant stone angels. The names on the gravestones were indistinguishable. Her feet were bare and she was trying not to step on the graves. She was looking for David. And it troubled her deeply that she couldn't find him anywhere. The sobbing brought her back to her bed. Over coffee she would tell herself that David was with the trees. He was where he wanted to be. His ashes had nurtured the forest he loved.

And then a new day would begin again.

• • •

As Grace was paying for the sleeping bag the plastic bottle of morphine fell out of her purse and dropped to the floor on the far side of the glass counter. The man stooped to pick it up. Reading the label he handed it back to her.

"Strong meds, eh? Gotta be careful with that stuff. It'll have you hooked faster than my jitterbug can catch a bass."

"Thanks." Grace feigned a smile.

"I had one head splitting ear ache last winter. Doctor said if he hadn't caught it I could have lost my hearing. The pain was un-be-leave-able so he gives me the demurral. Now that's a nice one. Yup sure was fun! Didn't feel a thing. Not a thing. So who's the bag for anyway?"

Grace said the first thing that came to her mind.

"Oh that's a surprise."

"Surprise?"

"Yup, a surprise."

• • •

When Grace told Jason and Bryan that she was moving back to her home town they threw a huge surprise party for her. Every artist in the west end came out, every patron and every friend, and even some not so popular but necessary folks were invited as well.

There was so much wine consumed that the empties filled five milk cartons that they left out on the curb the next day. That night Grace met a woman who was a friend of a friend. Her name was Allyson with a "y" and she and Grace hit it off like fireworks. They had so much in common. They each had an older sister with kids and an absentee husband. They had both been hitch hikers in the seventies; they secretly loved ballroom dancing but wouldn't dare tell anyone.

Grace was only sorry that they hadn't met earlier. She invited her to come and visit once she got settled in the hometown but something in

Allyson's eyes suggested it might not happen. And when Grace discovered that she worked for an agency that took in stray dogs, she gave her David's well worn sleeping bag. It seemed like the right thing to do - at the time.

• • •

Grace glanced back at the moose in the Bulls Eye Sports Shop and shook her head. A taxidermist would be appalled, not to mention the moose.

On the corner was a huge blue St. Vincent de Paul Used Clothing drop off bin. Grace went back to her car and opened the trunk. On the floor was the suitcase she had packed with the five days worth of clothes still neatly folded inside. Grace hauled the suitcase over to the bin, opened it up and carefully slid each piece of clothing into the mouth of the bin. She took the empty suitcase and tucked it behind the bin. Done.

There was one thing left to get – tequila. Grace looked across the street and exactly opposite of where she was standing was the store she had been looking for - SAQ - Vin, Alcool, Spiritueux. She crossed over to the other side. The door opened automatically and Grace walked through.

43

THE PUNGENT ODOR of alcohol soaked cardboard mixed with an ammonia tainted floor cleaner hit Grace's nostrils and sent her head swimming. With one hand on liquor store counter of the other hand over her mouth Grace felt the bile rise in her throat. And then the room started to swirl. Grace hit the floor.

Nothing. Nothing at all. Absolute nothing - a state of not being, of not knowing. A complete and utter void engulfed Grace. Slowly Grace opened her eyes and stared up at the face of the SAQ employee who was staring back at her. How had everything disappeared? And for how long? Grace had no idea how she had blacked out and she had no idea where the hell she was.

The woman in the blue denim shirt and precisely pressed jeans spoke to her but it sounded like gibberish or pig Latin.

A wave of panic flushed over Grace. "Where am I? What happened? Who are you?"

"That's what I'd like to know." The woman in her mid forties spoke with a thick Quebecoise accent. "Who are you? And why are you falling over like this? You're not even drunk or anything."

She reached down and took Grace by the elbow. "Maybe you should go and sit over here." The woman gestured toward an old stained wooden chair that had been placed beside a case of cheap sherry.

"So who are you?"

"I don't know." The fog was slowly lifting from Grace's hazy state.

"You don't know who you are?"

"Yes, I do. I do. It's just that I don't know where I am. Why am I here?"

"Look I'll get you a strong cup of coffee, double cream, double sugar, and you and I, we're going to figure this out."

• • •

"It's abnormal."

The doctor sat looking at an image on his computer. Grace stared at the doctor.

"How abnormal?"

Grace felt unsure. Were there degrees of normal and abnormal? Could she maybe have a little bit of a tumor like the size of a lentil or was it a big grapefruit sized one.

"The dye." The doctor continued to stare at the screen and fiddle with the mouse. "The dye gets absorbed more by the abnormal brain tissue."

"Guess I shouldn't have been dying my hair these past ten years." Grace tended to make jokes when things got too serious to handle.

"It's not looking good." Then the doctor turned to face Grace. His glance fell to the floor. "We can't operate at this stage."

Grace looked at the floor too and after that every word the doctor said disappeared into the hum of the incandescent lights that glared down from the ceiling above.

• • •

Grace fumbled around in her purse and finally pulled out her sunglasses. The harshness of the overhead light seared into her forehead.

She put the dark shades on. The woman handed Grace the mug of coffee. It had a cartoonish decal of a fisherman catching himself in the back of his pants with his own lure.

"You're not from around here. I know everybody here. And you're not one of the other summer folks with a cottage on the river. I know them too. I know everybody probably because I am related to half the folks up this way and my husband is a cousin of everybody else. Funny, eh? So, where you from anyways?"

Just then the electronic door swung open and the woman went to help a burly man in the camouflaged coat and florescent vest. She spoke to him in her best broken English while he picked up a two four of beer.

"Don't you go shooting each other up at that camp of yours. They going to have to fly you out in that there helicopter like they did with that guy last year. Hunt first, drink later. Not the other way around."

The man assured her in a teasing tone that they were men who knew how to be men and she didn't need to tell them what to do. Then he went out through the exit door leaving behind a trail of mud on the newly washed linoleum floor. The woman shrugged and muttered something under her breath - something about a tabernacle which to Grace's memory of high school French sounded distinctly like a religious curse. The woman spoke to Grace, "So like I said where are you from?"

By this time Grace realized where she was and she did not want to tell the woman anything about anything. Not a thing.

"I just came from the Sports Store."

"I know that. I see you pull up with your muddy car over there. I see everything, let me tell you. I don't miss a beat. No way. What I mean is where are you coming from? Where's home?"

"I 'm moving."

"Oh, moving? Where from?"

Grace looked at the woman and smiled and then told her a bold faced lie with as strong a sense of honesty as she could muster. "I come from a little place down on Lake Erie, Dunnville." Grace redirected the conversation. "Well, you have been so kind to me. I just came in to get some tequila."

"No one here buys tequila except for those born again hippie kids up back of Wakefield. "You going there?"

"No. Not this time."

Grace paid for the bottle and thanked the woman once more for her kindness.

The woman watched from the door as Grace went out and she called to her, "You think maybe you shouldn't be driving?"

Grace waved good-bye as she got back into her car, turned on the engine, and drove out of the north end of town.

44

A GREY BANK of clouds to the east shifted in the autumn winds and the sun streamed through them like the hand of God. To the west the rolling landscape undulated in a blend of gold, green, grey and blackish-brown. Nature's canvas invited Grace to sail on through, to be a mere speck on the planet, to suspend time, and just be.

She pulled the car over to the right and shut the engine off, her ears still humming from the sound of the motor and the rolling of the tires on the dirt road. The sizzle of silence filled her head. All seemed right for Grace. She would not be a burden to anyone.

This land would be her final resting place. And while it was not the rain forests of the Queen Charlottes it would be where David might find her if he were able to venture out on one of his earthbound journeys. There is peace in this land, thought Grace. There is peace.

• • •

From what seemed to be hugely high up in the bough of the apple tree, ten year old Grace glanced over the acres of hay in the abandoned farmer's field. The golden plants swayed to the rhythm of the wind like the waves on a mighty ocean. She was a pirate sitting in the crow's nest of an ancient sailing ship looking for a treasure island. Her spyglass was a discarded roll of cardboard from the left over Christmas wrapping paper. She held it up to her eye and scanned the fertile sea looking for a clue.

Out here on the briny sea she couldn't hear them fighting. Out here her father cursing about his right to drink if he wanted to couldn't hurt her ears. And her mother's shouting that she was going to leave him was far, far away in some other land belonging to someone else and not to Pirate Grace.

Suddenly a rabbit hopped above the height of the hay and then back down. Hopped up and back down, up and back down. Grace called to her invisible sea mates. "Ahoy. Land ahead. All hands on deck." And she scampered down the tree and raced out to where she thought the rabbit had been.

From the middle of the field she looked out in all four directions. No rabbit - nowhere to be seen. "Come out you stupid rabbit," she shouted. "I know you're out here. I'm going to make rabbit stew out of you stupid god dam rabbit. I hate you."

Grace slumped onto her knees. Tears rolled down her cheeks.

• • •

Grace glanced ahead. Slowly she brought the car to a stop. There in the middle of this dirt country road was a squirrel and a crow doing some sort of weird dance. The squirrel had an apple core in its mouth and the crow was hopping all around the squirrel. The squirrel dropped it and ran away until the crow began to peck at it. Then the squirrel flicked its tail and ran circles around the crow until the crow dropped it, half hopping, half flapping away.

Just then, coming toward them and toward Grace was a huge truck with a load of logs. The squirrel practically flew into a pine tree on one side of the road and the crow swooped onto a branch of a gnarly oak on the other side. When the rumble of the truck passed by and disappeared into the kicked up dirt Grace put the car into gear and drove away. She glanced in the rear view mirror. The crow and squirrel were on the road again doing their little dance.

• • •

Terry had come over around seven to pick up Grace. His hair was greased back and he smelled like he'd over-doused himself with Old Spice. It was the night of the spring dance at the high school. Grace had on a second-hand yellow floral dress that her mother had picked up at the Sally Ann. It made Grace feel grown up at fifteen and her budding breasts fit it perfectly. She was in the bathroom putting on her first tube of lipstick when he arrived.

Grace's father stood in the doorway of their post war house holding the wooden screen door open with one hand, a beer in the other. "You have her back before eleven you hear. Before eleven or I'll be out to find you."

Grace slipped under her father's arm. "Bye daddy."

"Be good, you hear."

"Yes, daddy."

At the dance the band mostly played covers of British music, the Beatles, Eric Burden and the Animals, and the Rolling Stones. All through 'Good-bye Ruby Tuesday' Terry held Grace and moved his hands up and down her back. She buried her head in the crook of his neck and slowly caressed his shoulders. That's when they decided to leave early.

On their way back to Grace's house they stopped to sit on a bench by the creek in the park behind the school. Terry put his hand firmly on Grace's breast and kissed her so deeply she thought that her body would explode. Then he took her hand and gently put it down the front of his pants. Time disappeared and so did they into the bliss of their ecstatic discovery.

• • •

Grace looked at the gas gauge. The indicator was already in the red just below empty. She knew she'd never make it to the park north of Maniwaki, let alone to the town itself. Besides she had no more money for gas. She'd spent it on the sleeping bag and the tequila. The last of her loose change went into a charity box beside the cash register at the SAQ.

As she pulled over to the side of the road again, she looked slightly ahead and across to the other side. Standing down a small embankment, was a weather beaten house. Its faded wood siding and boarded up windows could barely be seen through a stand of pine trees. Grace looked both ways and then drove over to the other side where the overgrown tracks of an old driveway still remained. She pulled in and the car jostled over the bumpy terrain. Grace saw that she could drive behind the house and out of sight from anyone who might drive by.

Her heart beat like a drum in her chest. This will be fine she said to herself. This will be just fine.

45

THE BACK WALL of the old farmhouse looked weather worn and rotting from years of neglect and abandonment. Loose wires from what once served as an outdoor light dangled above the wooden door. It swung precariously on one rusting-out hinge. Grace stepped out of the car and peered into the house through a window that was caked and smudged with years of dust and grit. In the dimness of the light she could make out what looked like an old wood stove and there seemed to be broken bottles on the floor.

This was not part of the plan. This was not the forest north of Maniwaki. This was some dilapidated old farm house where, by the look of things, teenagers came to get drunk.

Grace took hold of the latch to the back door and pulled it toward her. It swung open and then fell completely off its hinge hitting Grace on the shoulder on its way down to the ground. Shit. Oh bloody shit. The shock was greater than the pain. Grace wiped the paint chips off her coat and stepped into the house.

Cracked floor boards lay beneath the ripped up floral linoleum. Stained kitchen cupboards hung empty and over in one corner sat an old chesterfield with busted springs and stuffing scattered everywhere. Strewn on the floor amid the broken bits of beer bottles were a dozen or more old black and white photographs. Grace picked a few up and took them over to the window to see them in the light.

Two women dressed in furs stood between a man in uniform and all three of them were leaning up against the bumper of a 1930's vintage car. The smiles were vibrant and young. Another picture showed a picnic with everyone eating corn on the cob. The women wore hats and the men had on white shirts and suspenders. They all resembled scenes from some silent movie Grace had once seen at a film night back in the seventies when she was going to the Art College.

Grace wondered what had happened. The people in the photographs were frozen in time and hauntingly happy - hauntingly happy in a dismal decaying house. What had happened here - in this house? Where had everyone gone? Why did they leave and not take the photographs with them? Why had no-one come to take care of the house? Someone took the photographs. Someone cared. Once.

• • •

"Smile. Smile." The singsong voice was coming from the school photographer whose disembodied head was masked by his camera.

Grace did not want to smile. Her new teeth hadn't quite come in yet and she looked like a jack-o-lantern. All her classmates said so. Pumpkin face. You're a silly pumpkin face. And they threw dandelions at her out on the schoolyard during recess.

Grace's teacher spoke impatiently. "Look Grace would you at least stop scowling. You don't want an unhappy picture to take home now do you?"

So Grace smiled a broad toothless smile and after the flash had gone off she stuck her tongue out at the photographer. For that Grace was given the dunce hat to wear and was told to stand with her face to the corner.

But when the teacher wasn't looking Billy Wilcox gave Grace a stick of bubble gum. The next day Grace gave Billy her baking soda submarine.

Some people like Billy knew the meaning of injustice even at the age of seven and for that Grace bonded with Billy right away.

Sometimes they'd swap sandwiches and sometimes they'd draw pictures in the sand. But then one day Billy didn't come to school. A barrel-chested man in an oversized grey suit came and told the class that Billy wouldn't be coming back - ever. He had drowned on the weekend in the creek back of his place. Billy was dead.

That night Grace dreamed that she and Billy were riding horses at the county fair. His was white and hers was a palomino. Billy's horse went up into the air and Grace's horse followed right alongside. Together they swooped over the tree tops and skimmed the roofs of the houses on her street. When Grace finally landed on the ground Billy's horse was there but Billy was gone. Grace woke up sobbing, her pillow soaked with tears.

It was then that Grace in her complete innocence of knowing understood that her time on the earth was only a passage and that one day she would ride up into the clouds too. One day she would be able to be as free as the wind and be as bright as a shining a star because Billy had become one. This she knew.

• • •

Grace could see by the changing light that the day was wearing on. It would soon be night fall. This didn't leave her much time to do what she needed to do.

The car would be found if she left it in the open. About a hundred yards back from the house was a shed and further back from that, the remains of an old barn. Grace got in the car and turned the key. The car sputtered as the engine turned over. Grace backed up and then put the car into drive. Slowly and cautiously she steered the car across the rough ground to the edge of the barn. This will do fine she thought.

Grace got out of the car and went to the barn doors. She pulled them open. A rusting tractor from bygone days was parked in front of an old threshing machine. There was no room in the barn.

46

THE SMELL OF moldy hay hovered in the darkness of the barn. Grace looked around. She couldn't chance leaving the car where people would see it - at least not from the road.

Grace wandered deeper into the barn and peered into what might have been an old horse stall to the left of the tractor. There, lying on the ground was a huge canvas tarp. Grace watchfully reached for it, and pulled it slowly toward her for fear that a rat might come scurrying out. And when it didn't happen she realized she had been holding her breath the whole time. She gave out a huge sigh. "Crazy fool," she said out loud. "Buck up."

Grace dragged the canvas outside and around to the far side of the barn where there was a pile of broken windows, and odd slabs of wood leaning up against the wall of the barn.

• • •

The night the barn burned down everyone came out to watch it go up in flames. The orange, yellow and blue flashes flickered like fireworks and lit up the entire night sky. It was the biggest fire Grace had ever seen – bigger than the pep rally bonfires before the high school football games when effigies of the other school's team were torched to cinders.

Even in grade six Grace was allowed to go as long as Faye took her. And Faye unwillingly did so.

At least the horses got out safely. The firefighters said so and as far as they could tell no one was hurt but Grace knew it meant there'd be no more trail riding at the Anderson's Farm.

Mrs. Anderson had always been the guide but she hadn't been around for months. Some of the kids said she ran away. Said she met a man from the hardware store and he took off with her in his VW Beetle. Some said she was coming back. Others said they doubted it because Mr. Anderson had a younger woman helping with the horses and one of the kids even said he saw them making out in the barn.

Grace listened but it didn't really sink in what had happened until the next morning when the cop cars pulled up outside the Anderson's house. He's gone missing too, they said. Gone up, thought Grace, gone up into thin air like the smoke from the ashes of his barn.

• • •

Much to Grace's amazement, it had worked. The tarp covered the car perfectly, as if by some divine plan God had put it in the barn for her to discover. The discarded window frames and planks of wood provided a perfect anchor to keep the tarp from getting caught in the wind. Grace flopped down on an old stump, exhausted from the effort it took to hide the car.

Then she heard a car door slam. Then another. And another. Someone was there. Jee-zus Murphy, no. No.

Grace could hear hooting and cajoling and swear words coming from the direction of the house. Without thinking she ducked down and crawled on all fours along the ground to the end of the barn where she could barely see the house.

Five teenage boys started throwing stones at the already boarded up windows. One of them saw that the door had fallen off its hinges. He jumped on it over and over again until it snapped under his feet and the others called him a freakin' nerd when one of the pieces flew up and hit him in the face. Pushing and shoving each other they disappeared through doorway. A million "what ifs" rushed through Grace's mind.

Move feet, she silently screamed. Move.

Grace grabbed the sleeping bag, her well worn travel bag, the shovel and the saw she'd taken from her home, and headed across the open field toward the forest on the other side. Please God, she whispered, don't let them see me. Don't let them see me.

• • •

Two years after the barn burned down all that was left were the charred timbers and the outline of the stalls where the horses once stood. Grace had gone over to see the remains. She was fourteen and her PMS had exploded in a fit of rage when her father refused to give her money to go bowling that Saturday. They didn't have the money, he said. Right, said Grace. But you've got money for booze. And then he slapped her across the face.

Grace ran out the back door and kept running until she came to the concession road where the Anderson Horse Farm used to be. Someone new had moved into the house but the car was out of the driveway. Grace decided it was safe to go out to where the barn had once stood.

The hay was long and full of morning moisture. As she made her way to the barn the bottom of Grace's jeans got wetter and wetter with each step. She picked up a fallen tree branch and began to poke around at the bits of burnt wood. And then she saw them right on the perimeter of the barn floor, three small trees growing out of the ashes. Three maple keys had managed to take root and were flourishing in the ruins of the fire.

• • •

Grace made her way across the uneven ground of the field. She kept looking back to make sure she was still masked by the barn and that the house was out of sight. If she could not see the house chances were the boys wouldn't see her. Suddenly Grace's right foot went straight into a rabbit warren and she fell sideways, twisting her ankle on the way down. She bit her lip to prevent herself from yelling out an obscenity.

It isn't supposed to be like this. It isn't supposed to end with me killing myself by accident. I am doing it on purpose for crying out loud. And the paradox of her situation made her laugh and cry and cry and laugh - partly because the pain shooting up her leg was excruciating and partly because it all seemed to be going the wrong way.

Grace reached for her purse, zipped it open and dug around for the vial of morphine. Where I'm going there won't be any more pain, she said to herself. No more pain, no more running, no more, no more, no more. Grace took two capsules, gathered everything that had gone flying with the fall. She put her weight on her good foot and stood up.

A gust of wind blew through the branches of the nearby forest and they beckoned for her to enter in.

VI

But he himself went a day's journey into the wilderness, and came and sat down under a juniper; and he requested for himself that he might die...

1 Kings 19:4-5

47

THE SWEET SCENT of pine and moist moss encircled Grace. Little by little she climbed over and around the fallen branches and pushed aside the scraggy underbrush. The morphine had already started to mask the pain of her swollen ankle. It was also making it more and more difficult for Grace to keep moving. I must, she told herself. I must.

And so Grace moved deeper and deeper into the mystical realm of the forest until at last she could see nothing but trees in every direction. Looking up into the cathedral arches of the boughs a chickadee flit from branch to branch welcoming Grace to the protective embrace of the falling leaves.

Then she saw it - her final resting place. There, in front of her, was a natural depression in the land just beneath a towering pine tree. The needles had fallen and lay in a soft shimmering green sheet upon the forest floor. Two branches full of fresh pine needles were only a few feet away. They probably had been blown down in a wind storm, thought Grace. Thank you, God, wherever you are. Thank you, she said out loud. Thank you.

Grace unfurled the sleeping bag and lay it down on the ground smoothing it out with her hands. She looked at the tools she had brought with her to cut down branches. She set them aside. The tree had provided all that she needed.

Pulling out the tequila, Grace flashed upon those twenty something years of the all night parties. She unscrewed the cap and took a swig. The burning alcohol made Grace whoop like a coyote. She sputtered and coughed as the fiery sensation oozed down her throat.

Through the dense foliage to the west Grace tried to focus on the red flickering sunlight. It was a fire in a giant's hearth, thought Grace. I am Gretel. But I do not want to be found. Not by the living. Not while I am still breathing.

From her purse Grace took hold of the vial of morphine and dropped several more capsules into her mouth. With another swallow of the tequila she downed them. Again the heat of the alcohol seeped its way into her body. "I am coming to you David," she called out. "I am coming to be with you. Can you hear me?"

The whispering trees called back in voices that hummed in the harmony of a children's choir. "I know," she cried. "I know my sweet. We will be together soon." Grace gazed around and the bark on the trees started to shape shift. Gnarly faces looked at Grace and Grace looked back.

Grace took another sip, then another. The intoxicating warmth surged through her body like a sugary liquid coursing through the maple trees. And then another swig along with two more capsules of morphine.

The trees swayed. Or was it Grace? She kicked her shoes off, rolled her socks down and pulled them from her feet. Carefully she tucked each sock into the toe of each shoe. Grace unzipped her jeans and stepped out of them. She pulled off everything – her nylon jacket, her wool sweater, her purple turtleneck and finally her bra and her white cotton underpants. The breeze brushed by her nakedness and Grace began to wave her arms in the air.

"I am free, she sang. I am free, David."

Struggling to keep her balance Grace meticulously folded every piece of her clothing and put them in her travel bag. She stuffed her purse and car keys into the bag as well and then pulled a note out of the side pocket that she had written several days before leaving her home and placed it underneath the bag. On the blank piece of paper she had written – "This is my choice."

• • •

The Hunters' Moon shone down on her that night. Grace lay curled up in the sleeping bag, motionless and still with the large pine branches protecting her body. Grasped in her right hand were two acorns and in her left hand a photograph of David. She had taken it on one of their walks through the rain forest behind their home on the Queen Charlottes.

That evening no-one noticed the shooting stars that soared above where she lay, and no-one saw the burst of light that ignited the night sky when at last their two souls became as one again.

And the seasons came and the season went.

And in time the oak trees took root.

About the Author

Author Deborah Dunleavy is a connoisseur of the written word who takes joy in the natural music of language and how it shapes landscapes for the reader. She is an award-winning storyteller, author, and recording artist who is moving from children's literature to adult novels with The Truth About Trees.

Dunleavy, along with her husband and composer Howard Alexander, are the recipients of a grant from the Canada Council for the Arts given to write Isobel Gunn, an adult storytelling oratorio for orchestra. She lives in eastern Ontario where she enjoys writing, going for walks, and sitting by the dancing flames of a wood stove on a cold winter night.

Made in the USA
Charleston, SC
15 August 2015